MW00465158

Night Of Love

by John M. Haffert

This is a book about night vigils
begun by Our Lord (see page 23),
to help turn back the tide of evil.
They are nights of conversion and grace.

(Original printing, 1966, with Imprimatur of
Bishop George W. Ahr, S.T.D., Bishop of Trenton)

Revised Edition
Printed in the United States in 1997 by:

The 101 Foundation, Inc.
P.O. Box 151
Asbury, New Jersey 08802
Phone: 908-689 8792
Fax: 908-689 1957

ISBN #   1-890137-02-2

This

Night of Love

is dedicated to

the Sacred Heart of Jesus
and the
Sorrowful and Immaculate Heart of Mary

in reparation
for my sins
and the sins of the world.

Night Of Love

Night Of Love

Chapter 1.

A THOUSAND SOULS

Have you ever thought that during one night you could save a thousand souls?

It became a common belief among vigil groups (for a reason soon to be explained) that for every person making an all night vigil, a thousand souls, who would otherwise be lost, would receive the grace of final contrition.

At the first all night vigil to be held in New York City in May of 1969, Father Armand Dasseville, O.F.M. Cap., who at first may have thought this belief an exaggeration, exclaimed at the close of that first vigil at St. John's Church (next to Madison Square Garden in New York) to some two hundred tired but spritually invigorated vigilers:

"I feel indeed that for everyone who made this vigil tonight, a thousand souls were saved."

Twenty-five years and 300 all night vigils later, at the special 25th anniversary vigil in 1984 he said: "If the Lord were to speak from the monstrance tonight He would most likely paraphrase what He once said to the centurion: "I have not found such faith in so long a time!"

Cardinal O'Connor, the Archbishop of New York, was the special speaker at that golden jubilee vigil at St. John's. His Eminence said to the persevering vigilers:

"When the apostles went out on their first mission, they were very excited about the miracles they could work. But they were frustrated that they couldn't drive out certain demons. Our Lord told them, 'this particular demon can only be driven out with prayer and fasting.' That is the secret the vigilers realize, and the Church owes all of you a great debt...not only the Church in New York, *but the universal Church.*"

Spread of Vigil in City Seemed Impossible

Yet not one church in New York, of the several contacted, would even consider having a vigil back in the decade of the sixties. "Who would come? Who would risk being out in the city at night and going home in the early hours of the morning? Who would provide security?"

Does that sound familiar?

Finally one church had the courage to begin. It was St. John's, a church then scheduled for demolition!

The results were amazing. The very first night there were over 200 vigilers. Month after month the numbers did not diminish but gradually increased! The once moribund parish came alive. The church was renewed and *enlarged.* And little by little other churches began to hold vigils, including the most famous of all, St. Patrick's Cathedral.

"The vigils are called *A Night of Love,*" said Fr. Armand at the jubilee vigil at St. John's. "It is a night of prayer honoring the Two Hearts. The secular world naturally laughs and scoffs *but the all night vigil was in fact inspired by God.* The Old and New Testaments are replete with examples of night vigilers."

Example of Our Lord

How often we read that Our Lord "spent the night in prayer." The most famous night is the one before He died when He took three apostles aside with Him, called to them, awakened them. Could they not watch with Him?

In the five volumes of the life of Our Lord by Maria Valtorta one reads again and again that Our Lord, after giving the day to the world, often spent the entire night in prayer. One especially poignant example only a few weeks before His Passion was after Judas refused to change. As all were retiring for the night He said to the much tempted apostle:

"I will not sleep tonight. I will pray and wait for you." If the about-to-be traitor would but come to Him during that night, he would be saved. Without calling the attention of the others, He held back His Mother saying:

"I am staying to pray for Judas. Mother, will You help me?"

The Sacred Hearts prayed together as the moon crossed the sky and set, the first crowing of a rooster was heard, and then another, and gradually came the gray light of dawn. But Judas had not come.

Jesus looked at His Mother and said:

"You are pale, Mother. Great is Your fatigue...*God will make use of our prayer.*"

Almost at that very moment an old woman came out of a nearby house. She had been very helpful to Our Lord and the apostles in a hostile area. Greeting her, Jesus said: "May the Lord reward you."

She answered that she wanted no reward but there was one thing she would ask: That her husband would change. Although Judas had not responded, Jesus said at once to the good woman: "Go in peace. *It will be done to you as you wish.*" And her husband had the grace of conversion.

God does not force anyone's will. Judas became the traitor after *refusing* the graces poured out to him. But the all night vigil of Our Lord and His dear Mother was far from in vain. Indeed, only in Heaven will we know how many souls received the grace of conversion because of that one night of prayer.

Our Lord asked His Mother to join Him. For the salvation of many souls He asks US to unite our hearts to Her Immaculate Heart.

Blessed by John XXIII

The vigil movement was given great impetus at Fatima in 1960 when the Bishop of Fatima invited bishops around the world to participate in a vigil either at Fatima or in their own dioceses. Some three hundred bishops responded and elicited from Pope John XXIII, who participated in Rome, a cabled blessing: "To all who particpated in the all night vigil at Fatima, and *to all united with them in other parts of the world.*"

St. John's, in the very heart of Manhattan, became the first to take the risk of holding a vigil in New York City. And little by little other churches followed. And thus it has been around the world for the last four decades of the twentieth century.

Who would have thought that thousands of lay persons would give up a night's sleep, even though many would have to work the following day, to spend a night to honor the Sacred Heart of Jesus in union with the Heart of Mary? Who would have thought that *with virtually no urging from the pulpit* these multitudes would *seek out* churches holding these vigils?

Cardinal Heenan of London (Archbishop of Westminster) said:

"Until now it has been left to enclosed monks and nuns to watch and pray for the Church and the world. It is a sign of the awakening interest of the laity that ordinary men and women are now sharing the contemplation and the vigils." His Eminence continued:

"It is not difficult for Religious (monks and nuns) to arrange to spend a night in prayer. Lay people, and especially married people, must disrupt their lives to spend a night in prayer. They must be careful not to disrupt other members of the family...I wholeheartedly bless the self-sacrificing apostolate of the all night vigil."

Archbishop Thomas Pearson, S.M., said: "My own impression of All Night Vigils is that it is a work of a very high order, *especially suited to the needs of our day*...a generous act of continuous prayer and penance...a response to the invitation of Our Lady, *unalloyed with any mixed motives and a powerful antidote to selfish materialism.*"

There is no natural explanation for such unselfishness, such spiritual generosity at a time when Satan would seem to be more than ever the Prince of this world.

The explanation, which we are about to present, is a matter of the heart...our hearts and the Sacred Hearts.

This book (perhaps because it was one of the first) became a sort of "handbook" for vigilers. When the last printing was exhausted we heard of persons who made photocopies, and of copies repaired with tape and being used almost to the point of disintegration.

Particularly touching were two letters from an old priest and his housekeeper when their copies of the book were lost. Apparently one had forgotten to mention to the other about having written. The first letter, received a few days apart from the second, was from Rose Heil, of Wausau, Wisconsin:

"Dear Mr. Haffert: You do not know me but I feel I know you. For 58 years I have been keeping house for Father Herman Dietz. Many years ago we ordered two copies of *Night of Love* which we have been using for Holy Hours ever since.

"Last month I forgot to bring the books home with me from church. Early the next morning I went over before anyone came, but the books were gone. So I am writing for a special favor. Could you send us two more? The thoughts in this book are so helpful to make a good Holy Hour."

The second letter, from Father Herman Dietz, read:

"I have used this wonderful book for many years. Recently after making a first Saturday Holy Hour I left it in the church. Someone took it. It is so good, I suppose whoever took it, liked it and kept it. I am 91 and too old to make an all night vigil, so I make only a Holy Hour and make it daily."

Enclosed was a request for two books.

The Vigil is Like an Extended Holy Hour

The "thoughts" to which Fr. Dietz refers (in Part II of this book) are based on the mysteries of the Rosary. They originated not so much in front of a computer but in front of the Blessed Sacrament in the actual making of a vigil. And for those who cannot make a vigil, like 91 year old Fr. Dietz, a holy hour a day adds up to far more than one vigil a month. But for those who are able, "the night of love" is often the beginning of a new life.

Following is the testimony of some young people who explain how they came to make a vigil in the first place, and what happened as a result. Their experience (and it is *typical*) explains the growth of the vigils and why we say *it is a matter of the heart...our hearts and the Sacred Hearts.*

The first testimony is that of a young vigiler of the Holy Family Church in Artesia, CA.

Testimony of Ben DeGuzman

"It was eleven o'clock when my mom woke me up one evening to go to the Communion of Reparation vigil. Not only was I sleepy but a little angry with her for waking me. But she pleaded with me to come with her *even for ten minutes* to 'visit with Jesus,' as she put it.

"I already went to church Sunday. I try to pray every night. I am even a lector in our church. Wasn't this enough? I thought of myself as a pretty good person who loved and served the Lord. *What more can happen by going to this vigil?*

"Sleepy and, as I said, sort of angry, I was not about to go. But my mom seemed so pleading. And besides I did not want her to drive that late at night all by herself. I decided to go for her sake.

"I never expected it to change my life.

"That was two years ago and since then I have gone to the vigils every first Friday-Saturday except for the times we were away on vacation. I had never before understood loving with my "whole self" or what it is like to offer myself to God. Now *I have a completely new understanding of our Most Blessed Mother and Her Son, Our Lord.* To stay awake to adore Jesus and pray to Mary makes you realize how much you love Them.

What Keeps Me Going?

"Sometimes I ask, what keeps me going? Why do I keep coming?

"I often look around during the vigil. Why do these people come? Often times they come from work in their uniforms and they stay from 6 o'clock Friday evening to eight the next morning, then they go back to work. Ladies, with husbands and children at home sleeping, show up month after month, never saying

they are tired or wishing they, too, were home sleeping.
*"They are the ones who inspire me to love Jesus
and Mary through this devotion.*

"I sometimes forget how hard it was for me to come
that first time, how my mom had to beg me. I thought
I was doing her a favor. Yet now, because of her,
my life has changed. *I find myself looking forward to
the vigils. The First Fridays of the month come at a
time when I need them most.* A time when I stop
everything and come to talk with Jesus with my whole
body, releasing all the worries and challenges in my
life and offering it all to Him.

"Yet there is always a strong temptation to say:
'But not this time.' After all I am still young and
Friday nights are times to go out with friends or catch
up on precious sleep...*but the love of the Sacred Hearts
has had at least this one triumph, as I know They
will one day triumph in the world."*

Always a Temptation to say "Not this time"

There is one little sentence in the testimony above
that might be overlooked but which is typical. Ben
said that every first Friday he is tempted to say "Well,
just not *this* time...not *tonight."*

There seems always some reason why *this* night
should be an exception: The day was too tiring, there
is something scheduled early tomorrow, there is
something else I want to do tonight.

Although this temptation seems constant with every
vigiler, often at the last moment, vigilers respond to
the call of the Sacred Hearts.

Following is the testimony of Monica Street, of Dover,
Delaware, who writes:

"I was invited to the night vigils to the Two Hearts
but every time I would try to attend, something
invariably happened to prevent me from going. One
has to really *want* to go.

"I was finally able to make my first vigil in Dover
in June of 1995. And *seeing is believing!*

"Now, I am part of a team which promotes the
First Friday/First Saturday all night vigils in
Wilmington, our State capital. We started another vigil

at Our Lady of Fatima parish in New Castle with the permission of the pastor, Fr. Michael McDermott, who is now our Spiritual Director."

Another example is that of young Luina Dawn Capalla from Cerritos, CA., who writes:

Why I Have Changed

"My sister would always invite me when she went to the first Friday-Saturday vigils. But I was reluctant to deprive myself of sleep.

"After six months of watching her get ready every first Friday to spend the whole night in prayer, I decided to take her up on her offer and went with her *mostly out of curiosity.*

"At the evening Mass I was amazed to see such a large number of young people gathered in church on a Friday night. Not only did they sing beautiful songs that reawakened my awareness of God's presence, but after Mass, quite a number of them lined up for Confession.

"I usually see kids go to Confession with their mothers propelling them towards the Confessional, yet here were teenagers willingly lining up without adults prodding them! It was very inspiring.

"We recited the rosary and said the Nine Offices of the Sacred Heart of Jesus. Then we went to eat. Of course, some stayed behind for silent adoration. After the break, we went back to the church and recited the Chaplet of the Divine Mercy. Around 5 a.m., one of the priests led the procession of the Blessed Sacrament around the parking lot. At 5:30 a.m., the priest said the Mass of Our Lady and then we all went home. *Amazingly enough, I was not tired at all.* Was that one of the reasons my sister kept coming back?

Conversion Stories

"But then I began to learn the real reason. *I heard many conversion stories.*

"One guy used to belong to a band. He had very long hair and was an excellent guitarist. After becoming involved with the Alliance, he used his talents for God by playing at all the seminars and all-night vigils. Wherever they needed him, he went.

"Another story I heard was about a young man who belonged to a gang. He was notorious and many kids feared him. He became involved with the vigils and completely changed.

"My own conversion story is less dramatic. I continued to attend the all-night vigils but I thought it was mostly because of the friendly vigilers, the beautiful music they sang, and the pleasant 'break' when we enjoyed company and food.

"But I was beginning to pay attention to the God I had often ignored. *I realized how indifferent I, as well as many young people my age, have been in the presence of Jesus and Mary...*a presence we experience at the vigils. It was evident that we were doing something *important.*

"We knew about vicious crimes committed by our peers but now were made more aware of all the outrages, sacrileges, and indifference offending the Sacred Heart of Jesus. These outrages occur with more frequency each day, and the age of the perpetrators of these crimes gets younger. How can it change except by God's Grace?

"Now I know it is not enough to pray individually. Our times call for communal prayer and atonement *in order to change the hardened and indifferent hearts around us.*

"I am sure *this* is what attracted my sister...and this is why I have joined her and so many others in making Communions of Reparation. With the grace of God, I will continue to do so. Who knows...I may make others wonder what attracts me and then, as I did, come and see..."

Chapter 2.

WHAT IS THE GREATEST BENEFIT?

What would you estimate to be the greatest benefit of the all night vigils?

Would it be the saving of a thousand souls for every person making the vigil? Would it be personal conversions like that of Ben DeGuzman? Or a personal spiritual transformation like that of Luina Capalla? Would it be the ever increasing spiritual strength from each vigil, even each Holy Hour, with passing years to the very dawn of Heaven as in the case of Father Dietz and his housekeeper?

You are about to read of benefits beyond what you might even have begun to imagine.

Effect on Priests

Archbishop Gaudencio Rosales (Lipa, Philippines) says: "What truly touches me as a bishop is how these monthly vigils have *so tremendously affected the lives of our priests who have become involved.*"

One priest told him:

"Through the vigil Communion of Reparation I have grown to value deeply the Eucharistic-centered life-style. I have come to realize as never before that the real meaning of our Holy Orders is to safeguard the presence of the Eucharist here on earth. Through the vigil I have learned the beauty of victimhood essential in living a Eucharistic life-style. ...With 83 countries today legalizing abortion, how many souls do you think are already on the way to hell? I shudder at this horrible thought. Part of my priestly priority is to get them away from that brink *by making this reparation vigil.*"

We witnessed a similar effect of the vigils in the parish of St. John the Baptist next to Madison Square Garden in New York, staffed by a community of Capuchins.

As was mentioned in the previous chapter, the church was scheduled to be closed when the vigils began. And not only was the parish saved and the church enlarged, but the entire Capuchin community was deeply affected. The priests were so impressed, often even deeply moved, by the example of hundreds of laypersons spending a night in prayer, and by the Confessions heard throughout the night. Indeed it might be said that the wonderful effect on that Capuchin community was even more significant than the physical saving and enlarging of the church.

Major Feature of Vigil: Confession

Confessions are the major pastoral service of the vigils. Archbishop Rosales, speaking of the importance of the Confessions in the vigils (since Confession is one of the conditions given by Our Lady for obtaining Her first Saturday promise), said:

"In our Basilica of St. Sebastian, the Sacrament of Reconciliation takes a *major part* in the vigil program."

In Part II of this book, the first suggested program for vigils begins with a "penitential service" which is a preparation for Confession. Archbishop Rosales explains:

"We begin with the liturgy of the Word, then a short talk is given relating to the Sacrament of Reconciliation, initiating an examination of conscience by going over every Commandment and Captial Sin very slowly.

"A period of silence follows. In the meantime, ten or more priests begin to sit near the Communion rail just before the sanctuary. With meditational music playing in the background people begin to queue up before the priests for Confession." The Archbishop adds:

"This penitential program has amazingly made EVERYONE receive the Sacrament of Reconciliation *without exception* at every reparation vigil."

This Program is the Answer

Our Lady certainly foresaw the days when many would go to Communion without going to Confession for months on end. Of the many Communions today, how many are without proper preparation? How many are unworthy? How many even sacrilegious?

Our Lady said at Pellevoisin: "What *most offends My Immaculate Heart are careless Communions.*"

Even more than bad Communions, the Sacred Hearts are offended by *careless* Communions...by those who profess to love Them and do not prepare to receive Jesus in the Sacrament of His Love with careful examination of conscience and the Grace of priestly absolution.

So in coming to ask for a Communion of Reparation on the first Saturday, Our Heavenly Mother *required Confession*. And Archbishop Rosales exclaims:

"Just imagine the soul-cleansing received from this practice every month! If we consider the number of bad Confessions nowadays throughout the world because of lack of preparation, then *this program is the answer*."

Bad *Confessions?*

Yes, this is what Archbishop Rosales points out...that not only are there many careless and perhaps even sacrilegious Communions, but there are also bad Confessions. He adds:

"A bad Confession has been committed when the penitent, out of shame, consciously hides *at least one mortal sin* from the priest or confessor. Automatically it becomes an invalid Confession and if the soul receives Holy Communion, he or she commits a *sacrilege*."

But this is a *night of love*, and the graces of this night are such that it is to be hoped that even *perfect contrition* is possible to the vigilers. And perfect contrition makes possible plenary indulgences, which remove even all temporal punishment due to sin.

So how will we measure the benefits of the all night vigil of the Sacred Hearts? How will we measure this precious night of love on the days chosen by Their Own Sacred Hearts to draw us aside with them in Communions of Reparation...the first Friday and first Saturday...?

If we measure the benefits only in a good Confession and a loving Communion of Reparation, the benefits are deeper than the sea and higher than the highest stars.

Yet conversion, growth in holiness, salvation of souls...still are not the only benefits of this first Friday-Saturday Night of Love.

13.

Chapter 3.

A NIGHT TO SAVE THE WORLD

Dr. Joseph Rotblat, the atomic scientist who won the 1995 Nobel prize, said: *"The only way for the world to avoid nuclear destruction is to END war."*

But since *wars are caused by sin,* according to Our Lady at Fatima, are we sure to have nuclear destruction? *How can there be an end* to war? *Could God Himself wipe out sin* without taking away man's free will?

The answer, which even teenagers are beginning to see, is that *we can save the world from nuclear destruction by making* **reparation** *for sin.*

That is what the Hearts of Jesus and Mary ask of us as we begin the third millennium. And that is what the vigils are all about. That is why they are important.

At Fatima, the Queen of the World prophesied annihilation of entire nations, but then said: *"to prevent this,* I will come to ask for **FIRST SATURDAY COMMUNIONS OF REPARATION."**

Jesus, Who 300 years before had come to ask also for Communions of Reparation *on the first Friday,* now appeared to Sr. Lucia of Fatima and said:

"The time is coming when the rigor of My Justice will punish the crimes of various nations. Some of them will be annihilated." And appearing with Our Lady, as She asked for the first Saturday Communions of Reparation, He said:

"Have pity on the Heart of your most holy Mother, covered with thorns with which ungrateful men pierce it at every moment, **and there is no one to make an act of reparation** to remove them." He also said:

"I desire that devotion to the Immaculate Heart of My Mother be placed alongside devotion to My Own Sacred Heart."

An all night vigil, from the first Friday evening to the first Saturday morning, would seem the ideal response to the Hearts of Jesus and Mary for reparation. It fulfills in a special way the wish of Our Lord: "That devotion to the Immaculate Heart of My Mother be placed alongside devotion to My Own Sacred Heart."

Ideal Response to the Sacred Hearts

It fulfills the desire of both of Their Hearts for reparation. Our Lord had asked St. Margaret Mary for a one hour vigil, from eleven until midnight, on Friday eve. And He promised salvation to those who would make a Communion of Reparation on nine consecutive first Fridays.

Now with an additional promise of Our Lady, and the request for the Communion of reparation also on the first Saturday, there is the worldwide response *to Their Sacred Hearts:* the all night vigil from the night of first Friday to the morning of first Saturday.

The Sacred Hearts *asked for only about an hour on each of those days. But a few generous souls cry out: "O, Beloved Hearts of my Savior and my Mother! Not just an hour, but the entire night!"*

Pope John XXIII said: "This is the cloister brought into the world!"

Fr. Armand Dasseville, O.F.M. Cap., explained:

"Night vigilers pray in reparation for the wrongs in society and to obtain special graces and mercy for a generally sinful and sick world. *The vigils identify with Jesus and Mary in the redemption of the world."*

Chastisement Prevented

It is doubtful whether many, perhaps even most, vigilers realize that they are lightning rods of God's Justice. In the three examples given in the previous chapter (and they are typical) not one made any reference to holding back a chastisement of the world. They spoke only of the graces obtained: The presence of God...contact with the other world...an experience of conversion...*an experience of the Love of the Sacred Hearts...*

But at Akita, after revealing that a great chastisement is "at hand" because of the sins of the world, Our Lady said:

"*So far I have been able to hold it back*...offering to the Father the sufferings of His Son on the Cross, His Precious Blood, and **beloved souls who console Him** and form a cohort of victim souls" (*Meaning of Akita*, p. 7).

Such is the importance of these vigils, a cohort of devout souls making reparation to Their Hearts on the days They have requested: the First Friday, the First Saturday. They are the beloved souls who console. Their Hearts so much offended.

A Thousand Souls A Night!

The belief mentioned at the beginning of this book, that a thousand souls are saved by each vigiler, is based on a true story told by St. Alphonsus Liguori, a doctor of the Church.

A nun, with whom the Saint was well acquainted, felt inspired one day to make a novena to save a *thousand* souls. But about half way through she thought that was too much to ask. About half way through the novena she was about to cut the number down when, at that moment, according to Saint Alphonsus, Our Lady spoke to her and said:

"Already because of this novena a thousand souls *who otherwise would have been lost* have received the grace of final contrition."

If a thousand souls could be saved by a half novena, how much more should we trust for the salvation of many souls for each vigil...each generous response to the *appeal of the Hearts of Jesus and Mary* on the first Friday and first Saturday...not only with the short time They asked for each of those days, *but with an entire night!*

Cardinal Slipyi, who was freed by the Russians during the Council, said a special Mass at Saint Peter's in Rome, on June 1st, 1966, for a group of English vigilers who had just spent the entire night in prayer. He had first met the vigilers at the Eucharistic Congress in Bombay, where they had walked twelve miles during the night to the Shrine of Our Lady in Bandra.

"Continue!" His Eminence said, repeating the word spoken previously to the vigilers by Pope John XXIII:

"Continue! ...May you increase all over the world to draw graces upon mankind!"

Chapter 4.

VIGIL WONDERS

As we said in the previous chapter, some all-night vigils are especially interesting. Some have "made history."

If some excitement isn't generated by the organizers during the night, Our Lord Himself comes into action almost as tangibly as the night He came out of the monstrance and showed His flaming Heart to Saint Margaret Mary.

One would go a long way to match the excitement felt by the first all night vigil in Russia, on the Russian feast of the Assumption, in 1965. Among the forty who went to Russia to spend a night in prayer, were several Anglicans, including an Anglican minister. The need for prayers for Russia proved a greater ecumenical bond than any dialogue.

Then there was the vigil on the border of Poland in May of 1966, millennium of Christianity in Poland when the Communist government had refused a visa for the Pope and for the vigilers. But a group from England and another from America met *"by accident"* in neighboring Czechoslovakia, found a church on the border, and shared a vigil with the local people which made news around the world.

Little miracles have come to be expected by vigilers as recounted by Henrietta Bower in her history of the vigils in England (see p. 158).

Special feasts are often the occasion of unusually interesting vigils, as when the first Friday or Saturday coincides with New Year's day, or falls on the 6th and 7th of the month to honor God, the Father (a vigil Our Father requested), or on the Feasts of the Sacred Hearts (the Friday and Saturday after the octave of Corpus Christi).

Special occasions and special places make for special vigils.

One of those special occasions took place in Rome on the occasion of the jubilee of the apparitions of Our Lady of Fatima in 1972. On that night an amazing prophecy was fulfilled.

On April 2, 1927, the saintly Bishop Prohaszka died. He was the founder of a large community of sisters whose mother-house, later confiscated under the communist regime, remains the city hall of Buda (the other "half" of Budapest).

A few days after his death the bishop appeared to one of the nuns (Sister Athanasia Pekar) and told her: "You are to witness that I am your father." He told her that as a sign:

"You will receive *this two Hearts Scapular* (and he showed her a brown scapular with a picture of the Sacred Hearts on the front) *in Rome, during the night, from a Bishop.*

Even though Sister Athanasia could not doubt her senses, this prophecy seemed nothing short of ridiculous. She was of the Byzantine rite without the scapular devotion. What would she ever be doing in Rome? And how could it be that *during the night* a bishop would enroll her in a "two Hearts Scapular"...something which at that time had never been heard of *anywhere* in the world?

But forty five years later Sister Athanasia (who was the last of her community to escape from the Communists and make her way to America) without any advance planning was at the all night vigil in Rome in 1972. And after midnight *the Bishop of Fatima himself enrolled Sister Athanasia in the brown Scapular on which was a picture of the Sacred Hearts, exactly as it had been shown to her in a vision forty five years before.*

Consecration To The Sacred Hearts

We mention this because an important part of the vigils is a renewed consecration to the Sacred Hearts of Jesus and Mary through the Scapular of which Sister Lucia of Fatima said:

"It is our sign of consecration to the Immaculate Heart of Mary," and at Pellevoisin Our Lady called the Scapular "My livery *and that of My Son.*"

(The full story, which is recommended reading at vigils, will be found in the book *Her Glorious Title.)*

Every vigil is a thrilling experience. Every vigil is with Jesus truly present in His Sacrament of Love. Every vigil is truly a night of love. That is why vigils ought to continue to gain in force.

In September of 1965, just before the convening of the last session of the Ecumenical Council, the U.S.A. Center of the Blue Army of Our Lady and the Reparation Society promoted all night vigils across the United States in which *eighty-eight dioceses joined* with a special vigil held in the Vatican Pavilion, at the New York World Fair.

Mrs. Henrietta Bower, who could be called the "foundress" of the English vigil movement, came over from London. A priest came directly from just participating in a vigil in Russia. The Bishop of Fatima came from Portugal. The Pilgrim Virgin was there. It gave great impetus to the vigil movement in America, with five consecutive vigils held from that first Friday-first Saturday night of September, to the vigil of New Year's day, for the triumph of the Council and world peace.

That was a special vigil because of its special purpose and special participants. And any vigil can be made similarly "special."

Some vigils in some churches may seem uneventful. There might perhaps be some dull and even soporific talks during the night. But *there is something special about the night itself...a* night "aside" with Jesus (as with the three apostles in the garden) and with Our Lady. This night of love is a response in depth to *both Sacred Hearts.*

Our Lord had asked for the first Saturday Communion of Reparation. And Our Lady asked for the first Saturday devotion, promising to "keep us company" as we meditated on the mysteries of the Rosary, went to Confession, received Communion, all in a spirit of reparation.

Two Great Promises

Indeed, if there is any one principle reason for the "wonder" of the vigil, it is the *promises of Their Sacred Hearts.* **And the vigil *facilitates* the obtaining of those promises,** the first of which is an unconditional promise of salvation. The second is the promise of the personal assistance of Our Lady at the hour of our death "with all the graces and aid necessary."

The first is a promise of dying in the State of Grace. The second is the promise of a *happy* death. And we fulfill ALL the conditions during a vigil: the two Communions of Reparation, Confession, meditation on the mysteries of the Rosary, with the intention of reparation to the Sacred Hearts.

Many are drawn by the promises, but it is LOVE which brings us back again and again. It is love which makes the night of love what it is.

One of the priests who was always very much in demand to speak at our vigils was the Reverend Walter Ciszek, S.J., author of *With God in Russia* and *He Leadeth Me,* a spiritual classic. *His cause for canonization is under way.* He said:

"It is a blessing that the vigil movement is spreading. People who devote themselves to the vigils are those ready for sacrifice. Sacrifice always brings results. In good time the Lord will act, hearing the faithful prayers offered Him. The work you are promoting is so essential. The Blessed Sacrament adored by people, praying in a group, depriving themselves of sleep, is pleasing to God. After my first talk to the vigil members, I became a member in spirit. *Several times a day, I pray for you and your group and for the movement. I believe in this movement, so necessary in our times."*

Chapter 5.

WHY FRIDAY? WHY SATURDAY?

There will be special vigils outside those which begin on first Friday once a month.

God the Father has asked for a vigil on the 6th day of every month (starting at 9:00 p.m. and ending at 6:00 a.m. on the 7th) with the intention that the Divine Father may be known, loved, and honored by all men. And the Father dictated specific meditations for the Rosary which will be found in the Appendix. So it is natural to have this special vigil when First Friday is the 6th day of the month.

We can also have special vigils beginning New Year's Eve (ending on the first day of the New Year, Feast of the Mother of God).

The Feast of the Sacred Heart is always a Friday, followed the next day (Saturday) by the feast of the Immaculate Heart of Mary. And when these feasts fall on the first Friday and Saturday a very special, well publicized vigil, can be planned.

Special Days Of The Two Hearts

We ALWAYS have the vigils on the first Friday-first Saturday, because these are the days They requested. They are days related in a special way to Their Sacred Hearts.

Friday was the day the Sacred Heart of Jesus was pierced for us as a fount of Mercy. Saturday was the day of the prolonged passion of Our Lady's sword-pierced heart, because Jesus was dead and the apostles were scattered.

It was the day after He confided His Church to Her from the cross, and where was Judas? Where was Peter? They would be devastated for having denied Our Lord. And what about all the other disciples who had fled?

Despite the sword piercing Her Heart, or because of it, She had to help them! She had to let them know that *She* forgave so they would know that *He*, even in the tomb, forgave.

This tragic first Saturday after the crucifixion reveals all the depths of the Sorrowful and Immaculate Heart of Mary, Coredemptrix, Mother of the Church.

That is why *Saturday* is Mary's day.

It was Jesus Himself who asked us to have pity on Her. "Your Mother," he said, pointing to Her thorn-pierced heart at Pontevedra when She made Her first Saturday request, "console Her."

And why did She ask that on this day we confess, meditate on the mysteries of the Rosary, pray the Rosary, and make a *Communion of Reparation for the sake of Her Immaculate Heart?*

Our Lady Herself told us in Her previous apparitions in Pellevoisin (which after more than 100 years were approved in 1984): "What *most offends My Immaculate Heart are careless Communions.*"

Careless Communions deeply offend Our Lord, Who pointed to His Heart flaming with Love when He asked for Communions of Reparation on the first Friday.

What offends the Heart of Mary is what offends the Heart of Jesus. St. John Eudes, who was responsible for introducing in the Church both the Feast of the Sacred Heart and the Feast of The Immaculate Heart of Mary said:

"Do not forget that not only does Jesus reside and dwell perpetually in Mary's Heart, but that He is in truth the Soul of Her soul. Therefore coming into the Heart of Mary means to honor Jesus, and to invoke Her Heart is to invoke Jesus."

What could more offend both Their Hearts than *careless* Communions? And yet how often I myself have received Jesus carelessly! And today, *when so few go to Confession* in comparison to the many who go to Communion, how many careless and even sinful Communions may there be?

Oh, what a need for reparation!

The vigil responds to that need!

We begin by examining our conscience for Confession, we strive for true contrition, and we immerse ourselves in the mysteries of their Sacred Hearts as did St. John Eudes when he prayed:

"O Jesus, living in the Heart of Mary, be the life of my heart! Mary, Mother of Jesus, obtain by Thy intercession, I beseech Thee, that I may have but one heart with Your Beloved Son and You."

And in return He heard Jesus say:

"I have given you this admirable Heart of My dearest Mother *to be one with yours* so that you might have a heart worthy of Mine."

Oh, as we prepare to receive Jesus twice in this night of love...may we hear Him address those same words to us! May we receive Him with Her faith, Her trust, Her love.

Then indeed shall He, and also our dear Mother, be consoled. The careless Communions of our lives, and those of many others, will be forgotten in that flame of love.

Our Lady said at Akita that so far She has been able to hold back the chastisement of the world by offering the Passion of Jesus to the Father, and by the cooperation of a few generous souls.

Let us be counted among them! And let us do our utmost to make their number increase!

(Note: If the first Saturday should be the first day of the month, the following Saturday is celebrated as the first Saturday, as Our Lord said the date of the first Saturday could be changed by any of His priests for a good reason, and since the first Friday cannot be changed, we are obliged to advance the first Saturday.)

Chapter 6.

OUR LORD BEGAN IT!

Although the idea of a night of prayer before the Blessed Sacrament came to the world three hundred years ago in a little chapel in Paray le Monial, France, when Our Lord appeared out of the monstrance and pleaded for reparation to Him in the Sacrament of His love, it was not until our own day that night adoration began to emerge from the cloisters and to become an organized movement among the laity.

Indeed, it would be more proper to say that only in most recent years, as a response to the appeal of Our Lady of Fatima for reparation, all night vigils have become an international phenomenon of faith.

How It Began

It became a custom to have the Blessed Sacrament exposed at Fatima all night on the vigil of the anniversary of Our Lady's appearances, because thousands of pilgrims came to Fatima on foot (sometimes walking five or more days) and had no place to sleep, except in or about the Cova of Fatima, before attending Mass the following morning.

On behalf of these thousands of pilgrims spending the night in the great natural amphitheater of Fatima, prayers and exhortations before our Eucharistic Lord sounded from the loudspeakers until Communion was distributed in the early morning hours to tens of thousands of joyfully tired pilgrims.

Pilgrims then began to come in increasing numbers to spend the entire night in prayer and reparation, rather than to come just the following morning for the Pontifical Mass and procession in celebration of the anniversaries of the apparitions.

It seemed that Our Lady, who had appealed here for reparation, was literally drawing people to Our Lord in the Blessed Sacrament for a night of sacrifice and prayer.

Then, as we have already mentioned, in 1960 an "official" recognition of the importance of the vigil came from His Holiness, Pope John XXIII.

This Pope had called Fatima the "Hope of the world," and it was he who had opened the last part of the Fatima secret *that same year.*

Could it have been because of the secret that shortly after reading it, His Holiness met alone with the Bishop of Fatima and the Bishop subsequently wrote to all the other Bishops of the world *to announce a special all night vigil of reparation at Fatima on October 13 of that year,* suggesting that the Bishops might like to do something similar in their own dioceses. Over three hundred bishops agreed.

After the vigil, Pope John sent a long, spontaneous cablegram to the Bishop of Fatima expressing gratitude and a special blessing on all who participated in this vigil, "not only at Fatima, but everywhere in the world." It is believed that Pope John himself spent that entire night before the Blessed Sacrament in union with the pilgrims at Fatima and in other places where hours of sacrifice and reparation were made.

A Worldwide Call

Meanwhile, even as at Fatima, Our Lady seemed literally to be drawing people to reparation before Our Lord in the Blessed Sacrament, She had already begun to do so in other parts of the world.

In 1954, Pope Pius XII proclaimed an extraordinary Marian Year. This compelled a devout and extremely competent priest in England to organize a national pilgrimage to the ancient shrine of Walsingham, which had once been the greatest Marian Shrine in the English Isles.

As at Fatima, it was at first necessary to remain without lodging because of inadequate accommodations at the shrine, which had been destroyed during the reformation, that an all night vigil became the object of the pilgrimage: a day up from London, a night of prayer before the Blessed Sacrament, and a day's trip back.

Those who made that pilgrimage were so overwhelmed with the return of love that Our Lord made to them from the Blessed Sacrament, that they were impatient to have an all night vigil again. In 1956 they chartered a plane to Fatima...paying all the expenses just to fly to the Shrine, spend a night, and fly back!

Since Fatima was so far away, they soon began going regularly to Lourdes.

Within ten years after that first vigil in Walsingham, 33,000 vigils were made in Lourdes by English laymen and women who paid for the plane flight, and took their weekend to spend a night at the grotto in sacrifice and prayer before Our Eucharistic Lord (see p. 159).

On one occasion when we met these vigilers at Lourdes, their leader, Mrs. Henrietta Bower, asked us to join her in the Stations of the Cross. She had spent the entire night in prayer and looked terribly tired. We knew that this extraordinary woman, wife of a member of the British Parliament and herself from a noble family, had caused THOUSANDS of persons to make the sacrifice of a sleepless night of prayer and penance because of the message of Fatima.

When we began that very long and very rocky ascent, Mrs. Bower took off her shoes. She walked barefoot over the sharp stones. So did we. Somehow we knew that, after a night of prayer and almost two days without any regular sleep, she was doing this with the fervent prayer that we might somehow extend the message of the All Night vigil to America, and we joined in that intention.

She later confirmed this when she came to America in 1960 when the vigil movement in America was launched simultaneously in 80 dioceses.

And so one can say it has been directly by the Grace of God that this wonderful movement has spread in our day as never before. (There has been a practice of all night vigils in the Church since earliest times, like the famous Easter Vigil.)

It should be noted that the All Night vigil is very different from the forty hour devotion, or nights of holy hours in which different persons take turns. A *full night is given by each person* from the opening evening Mass to the closing Mass in the morning.

One member of the all night vigil group from England, Mrs. Gladys Tower, said:

"It is no small thing to remain without sleep during and after a long journey by plane across the sea and most of France; all day and the entire night in Lourdes and part of the next morning, until the pilgrims finally reach home. Yet it has been done by thousands, even with enjoyment and in spite of adverse weather conditions; fear of accidents; irregular meals; and the gift of all one's time in Lourdes to Our Lady. *It was wonderful* is the usual comment to which is often added the story of a personal favor granted to pilgrims who put themselves and their requests last." Mrs. Tower sums up all the reasons which have compelled her and an increasing number of thousands around the world to give such a night of prayer:

"It is said that the penances the devil really fears are the curtailment of food, drink, and sleep. We know the little Seers of Fatima did all three, while St. Bernadette humiliated herself in the dust, when commanded by Our Lady to wash in the muddy water which is now the famous miraculous spring."

The main elements of a vigil are Holy Mass, procession of the Blessed Sacrament, procession of Our Lady's statue, stations of the cross, a coffee break, homilies, meditated Rosary, closing Benediction and Mass.

When done well, the program is so full that the night *doesn't seem long enough.* When not done well, it could be dull. Fortunately we have rarely seen it done other than well. As almost all vigilers will testify, there is a magic about this night with Our Lord, this night of truly fulfilling the greatest desire of our Mother expressed in every one of Her comings: FOR REPARATION.

But as in everything, one gets out what one puts in. And for a most successful vigil one should have a well prepared program and follow some tested guidelines.

Chapter 7.

SUGGESTED PROGRAMS AND GUIDELINES

The guidelines are simple: Have no LONG talks; involve the vigilers themselves; have a variety of intentions; focus on *a need of the moment* (such as an earthquake, war, a nearby abortion clinic, etc.); *involve the vigilers*, plan to include their movement. Most of those making this vigil with you are "saints." They have been living a Eucharistic life sometimes for many years. They have the Holy Spirit living in them. **And *they* are the key to a most successful vigil.**

You can involve them most easily by inviting each one to come up before the Blessed Sacrament to offer personal intentions.

If a microphone is available, set up a kneeler in front of the altar and invite them to HOLD the microphone as they offer their intentions. They are usually reticent, modest, very soft spoken. They will be speaking to Our Lord. But you want *everyone* present to be sharing in their intentions, sharing in their inspiration.

Invite individuals *to read parts of the meditations of the Rosary*, giving them a copy in advance so they will be prepared. And invite them to offer intentions which the Holy Spirit may inspire.

Invite them to do other *readings* according to your plan for the vigil.

It is good to say every other decade of the Rosary *standing*, with a short hymn (such as the Ave of Fatima or Lourdes, or the Stabat Mater, or "Come let us adore Him,") at the end of each decade. In a full vigil, other movement is provided by processions of the Blessed Sacrament and of Our Lady's statue, and the Way of the Cross.

Have a plan, even if it is not always the same. Indeed some vigils could honor God the Father, others the Holy Spirit, others to celebrate special occasions, special feasts, special intentions.

If you are a priest, invite one or more lay persons to help you with the plan. If you are a lay person, of course, coordinate your plan with the priest. Deacons can be especially helpful in vigils.

Any plan should follow the guidelines above, while following the inspiration of the moment. But the entire night should be planned so there are no long gaps, especially in the early hours of the morning.

If not a part of the plan, **the Chaplet of Mercy and the prayers taught by the angel at Fatima can be introduced at any time.** After the Mass of the Sacred Heart comes the act of consecration to Him, and at the Mass of the Immaculate Heart (preferably at the Offertory) enrollment in the Scapular and renewal of consecration to the Immaculate Heart of Mary.

How Long?

The ideal vigil is from 9 p.m. to 5 or 6 a.m. When the vigil is in a remote place and those attending must drive some distance to attend, the time may be from 9 p.m., to 2 a.m.

In some areas the night is divided into a series of Holy Hours. For example in the Church of Our Lady of Mercy in Albany, N. Y., the vigil for the first Saturday of October, 1966, was divided into Holy Hours on the following subjects:

1) Hour for the Conversion of Russia
2) Hour for the Conversion of Sinners
3) Hour for the Persecuted of the World
4) Hour for the Soldiers at War
5) Hour for Priests and Religious
6) Hour for Lay Apostles and Apostolates
7) Hour for the Poor Souls in Purgatory
8) Hour for Bishops, Priests, and Religious

There may be as many different programs as there are vigils and, as we said earlier, one should take advantage of special dates, special places.

We will propose two programs which we consider ideal: One for the shorter vigil (with a possible extension), and one for the full vigil.

Full Vigil

9:00: Penitential Hour. It is well to begin the vigil in this manner for several reasons. Essentially this is an examination of conscience, a review of the commandments of God and of the Church, a meditation on the horror of sin and the need for true repentance. Many books are available for this. Also one can use the new Catechism.

This is a preparation for the Confessions which will follow during the night, since Confession is an obligatory condition for the first Saturdays. And if the priest is invited to give this public examination of conscience, he will then be free during the time before the first Mass to hear Confessions.

9:30: Sorrowful Mysteries of the Rosary with suggested meditations which follow in Part II, praying that Our Lady gives us an appreciation of the night we are about to spend, and to prepare us for the Votive Mass of the Sacred Heart which will open our vigil

10:30: Mass of the Sacred Heart, since most vigils begin on first Friday, the sermon during the Mass should bring out the great appeal for love and reparation repeated by the Sacred Heart in our own time: "Could *you not watch one hour with Me?"*

The Blessed Sacrament is exposed.

Immediately after Mass the Blessed Sacrament is exposed. Hymns of the Sacred Heart and of the Blessed Sacrament are used throughout.

If the vigil begins at nine o'clock, there is now only an hour left before midnight for the Litany of the Sacred Heart, renewal of consecration to Him, and procession of the Most Blessed Sacrament

Be sure to include the Chaplet and the prayers taught by the angel at Fatima (adoring the Blessed Sacrament)

Many vigils cannot have the service of a priest the entire night, because of his obligations in the early morning, and in this event the Blessed Sacrament is left enthroned after the procession and the lay vigilers continue with the program through the night.

12:00: The Joyful Mysteries begin. We turn to the Immaculate Heart of Mary in this first hour of the first Saturday, to honor the Sacred Heart of Jesus even more. With ten minute meditations, the first three decades require about forty minutes. Then, still contemplating the birth of Our Lord and Our Lady's journey with Him to the temple, *we carry the statue of Our Lady in procession while singing the Lourdes or Fatima hymn.*

This procession will follow the same route as that of the Blessed Sacrament. It is usually down the center aisle, around and back on one side of the church, then back down the opposite side, returning to the altar by the center aisle again. It is always good to have the vigilers remain in the center aisle and separate, letting the returning statue pass between them.

Now we sing a stirring salute to Our Queen (such as "Hail, Holy Queen!") and kneel for the last two Joyful decades.

1:30: Coffee Break. This is an important part of the vigil, not just for refreshment but so vigilers can greet each other. We are here on a special calling of the Sacred Hearts.

However the break should not be more than fifteen minutes, with half the group going at a time, leaving the other half in adoration.

Since we have already said the Sorrowful Mysteries, we now have a sermon if a priest is present, otherwise a reading on the meaning of the Passion. This is followed by the Stations of the Cross. We sing the *Stabat Mater* in English between each station, and here it might be noted that it is helpful, especially in these morning hours, to have organ accompaniment.

In the case of a very small group, all can walk around the church for the stations. Usually only the reader, cross and candle bearers proceed to the stations.

Now follows a unique adoration somewhat similar to the adoration of the cross in the Good Friday liturgy. But since we have Our Lord exposed before us, instead of prostrating before a crucifix, *each vigiler goes to the altar steps, kneels on both knees, and bows almost until the forehead touches the floor. Meanwhile, the entire group recites over and over the Prayer of the Archangel, "O Most Holy Trinity, I adore Thee profoundly. I offer Thee the most Precious Body, Blood, Soul, and Divinity of Jesus Christ present in all the tabernacles of the world, etc."*

This act of individual adoration recalls the first great apparition of Fatima: the Archangel left the bleeding Host and the Chalice suspended in the air and *prostrated himself* before Them. His repeated recitation of the prayer was indelibly etched upon the minds of the three children so that, ever afterward, they remembered each word of the prayer and felt impelled to recite it often.

We recall that in the very second apparition of Our Lady, She permitted rays of light to stream from Her hands upon the children and they felt lost in God and cried together: "O *Most Holy Trinity I adore Thee! My God, My God, I love Thee in the Most Blessed Sacrament!"*

Now little more than an hour is left before the closing Benediction. This is the hour of greatest fatigue, therefore our best speakers ought to be saved for the Glorious Mystery meditations. And with ten-minute meditations, the hour passes all too swiftly, preparing us for the great climax of the Benediction and the Mass, usually *the Saturday Votive Mass of Our Lady or the Mass of the Immaculate Heart of Mary.*

Confessions Throughout

To obtain the promise of the first Saturdays one MUST make not only a Communion of Reparation on the first Saturday, but one must also (either on that day or within seven days) make a Confession of reparation. This means that even if one does not have any grievous sins to confess, one must receive the Sacrament of Penance in a spirit of reparation for all sins committed against the Immaculate Heart of Mary.

The only other obligation of the five first Saturdays has already been fulfilled during the morning with our Rosary and meditations.

If there should be more than one new vigiler present, *it is important to explain the first Friday/first Saturday devotion* which will be found in the next chapter. Different persons could be appointed to read it in parts. An alternative would be to lend them a copy of this book so they can read these first chapters.

Will Vigilers Avoid Purgatory Completely?

We may not be making this vigil because of the promise Our Lord attached to the first Friday Communions, or because of the promise Our Lady attached to the practice of the five first Saturdays. But the promise Our Lady made at Fatima for the five first Saturdays indicated not only the grace of a happy death, but that SHE WILL COME TO US AT THE HOUR OF DEATH. And this recalls the great experience of Saint Alphonsus Ligouri.

The saint wrote in the *Glories of Mary* about the promise of salvation and of speedy liberation from Purgatory which Our Lady attached to perseverance in the Brown Scapular. Then he added:

"If we do a little more than Our Lady asked, can't we hope that we won't go to Purgatory at all?"

When Saint Alphonsus was dying, he awoke from a coma, sat halfway up in bed with arms outstretched, and stared ecstatically to the fore. Then, as he whispered "Mary!" he sagged back on the pillows and was dead.

Forty years later, when ecclesiastical examiners opened the coffin, a strange sight met their eyes. All corruptibles in the coffin (except buttons, buckles, bones) had returned to dust, with one singular exception. There midst the corruption of the tomb in perfect preservation (even though made of highly corruptible wool and cotton) was the Saint's brown scapular, miraculously echoing the Saint's words: "If we do a little more than Our Lady asked, can't we hope that we won't go to Purgatory at all?"

The all night vigilers are not usually here for this glorious night of prayer and sacrifice for the sake of a reward, but because of love...because they still hear the words of Our Lord in the garden: "Could you not watch one hour with me?"—and the more recent words of Our Lady as She trembled over a terrifying vision of hell: "So many souls are lost because there is no one to pray and to make sacrifice for them."

Their reward is the joy of fulfilling Our Lady's wishes. Their reward is the joy of being together in the true presence of Christ, supported and buoyed by each other's faith. Their reward is in the act itself...the act of loving Christ in our midst, and of experiencing His love in return, at a time when the world's only hope lies in this love.

The above is only a suggestion. Make up your own hour-to-hour, minute-to-minute, program for your own next vigil, listing after each time segment the name or names of the persons who will carry it out.

The short vigil, ending at 2 a.m., would be the same as above until midnight. Then have the coffee break at midnight, followed by the Joyful Mysteries of the Rosary with Benediction at 1:15 followed by Mass of the Immaculate Heart. For persons not traveling from afar, the Blessed Sacrament may be exposed again after Mass and the rest of the program completed.

Since the Rosary is usually a very important part of every vigil, at the same time that we are aware of the true Presence of Our Lord before us, we should also be aware that when we pray the Rosary, Our Lady joins us!

Chapter 8.

IS ANYONE LISTENING?

When Blessed Jose Maria Escriva, founder of Opus Dei, asked, *"What is the first thing necessary for devotion to Mary?"* he himself answered:
"The first thing necessary is to realize that She is alive." We must realize that, assumed body and soul into Heaven, Her real motherly heart is beating with love for us and She is constantly waiting for our slightest response. *This is especially true when we wish to draw closer to the Sacred Heart through the mysteries of Her own Immaculate Heart.*
We need but LOOK at the Rosary and realize that *Our Lady Herself carried it* when She appeared at Lourdes and at Fatima. Why, except that *She longs to share with us Her mysteries?*

First Words at Lourdes

Bernadette was amazed at seeing Her in the grotto, beautiful but silent. At first *no words were spoken.* It seemed almost as though Our Lady were waiting for Bernadette to speak. Then noticing the Rosary on Our Lady's wrist, Bernadette took out her own Rosary and said the prayers...one after the other.
Still not speaking, Our Lady took Her Rosary and *counted the beads* with Bernadette. Only at the end of the decade did She speak at Lourdes for the first time. She then JOINED St. Bernadette saying: *Glory be to the Father, and to the Son, and to the Holy Spirit, as it was in the beginning, is now, and ever shall be. Amen.*
From the moment we take the Rosary in our hands, Our Lady is waiting to hear us and *to join our hearts to Hers in its mysteries.*

Her Special Sign

That is one of the special things about the Rosary; it IS REAL in our hands...Her gift which we can *see and feel.*

As a loving and knowing Mother, Our Lady did not just tell us to say certain prayers but *gave us this visible, real Rosary with which She Herself appeared in every vision of Fatima* asking us over and over to use it.

And there is another gift of Our Lady which is *real* and which *we can see and feel* and which She also held out to us at Fatima: **The Scapular.**

St. Claude, to whom Jesus chose to have St. Margaret Mary reveal the messages of His Sacred Heart, tells us of the great value of this gift of Our Lady to draw us into Her own Immaculate Heart. He says that even though the Church tells us, and the saints tell us, and our faith tells us: **"I need but reach out and TOUCH my Scapular, and *I* know."**

When asked why Our Lady appeared in the final vision of Fatima holding the Scapular out to the world, Sister Lucia said: "Because She wants everyone to wear it. *It is the SIGN of consecration to Her Immaculate Heart."*

It is a *sign* that Our Lady, in Her maternal love, is morally present with us. It is a *sign*, like the Rosary, that SHE IS WAITING TO HEAR our every word! We need but reach out and TOUCH it and we *know.*

Her Image

When we pray before the Blessed Sacrament, Our Lady is present in a most special way, because Her Heart is but one Flame of Love with the Sacred Heart of Jesus.

Still another way to help us realize that Our Lady is present to us by Her love and by Her intercession, is Her statue.

Like the Rosary and the Scapular, Our Lady's images are most helpful in *making us aware of Our Lady Herself.*

In the city of Rome there are more than one hundred images of Our Lady which have been crowned by Popes and which are called "miraculous" because of great favors obtained by persons praying before them. Not all of them are beautiful. Indeed, some very old ones are dark, and hardly beautiful at all. But they *represent* Her who is more beautiful than all other women. They *present* Her to us.

Doctor of the Church

St. Alphonsus, a doctor of the Church, tells us that when we go into church, we should first go to the Blessed Sacrament to visit Our Lord, and then *go to Our Lady's statue to "visit" Our Lady.*

The holy doctor knows that Our Lord is PRESENT when we visit Him in the tabernacle, but he reminds us that Our Lady's statue *represents* Her presence to us, a presence of intercession and love. And while we cannot have the real presence of Our Lord in the Eucharist in our homes, we can have statues of Him and of Our Lady which represent another kind of real presence: that of Their Love.

There is a fourth way both to be aware that Our Lady is listening when we say the Rosary and to show that we KNOW She is listening: *Have an intention for each bead.*

You are asking the all powerful Queen of Heaven to PRAY for you in each Hail Mary. For *WHAT are you asking Her?* Think of it! Before you begin each decade, THINK *in the light of that particular mystery,* what you want Our Lady to do for you, for someone you love, for the nation, for the world...

On the first Saturday of the month, during those fifteen minutes with Our Lady, thinking about the mysteries of the Rosary, think about all the treasures hidden in those mysteries FOR WHICH YOU FORGET TO ASK.

There is one intention which fits all the mysteries and which Our Lady seems to delight in hearing: "Send forth the graces of your Flame of Love to all mankind." As Our Lady of All Nations She asks us to pray that *now* Our Lord will send His Spirit over all the earth...that the Holy Spirit may live in all peoples, everywhere, "to preserve them from corruption, destruction, and war."

Part 2.

ALL NIGHT VIGIL MEDITATIONS
ON THE ROSARY

We have suggested a simple vigil program, which we especially recommend, based on the mysteries of the Rosary.

Obviously this program will be most successful if the ten minute Rosary meditations (which follow below) are well presented. They offer an excellent basis for the vigil especially when the priests would be busy with Confessions.

To add interest three or four persons can coordinate and take different parts of the same meditation. Also special intentions can be added. For example:

If we were meditating on the first Joyful Mystery with the intention of reparation for sins of abortion and other sins against the dignity of parenthood, someone could cite some statistics or current news events showing the evil and extent of sins of abortion.

It adds a great deal to a vigil if the intentions are current, such as prayers for persons killed that day, or week, in some disaster, prayers for drug addicts tied into some news event, prayers for youth threatened by pornography or violence; prayers to have a pornographic shop removed from a neighborhood, and on and on.

Indeed, if there were only four lay persons to conduct the vigil, each one of the four could take turns coordinating similarly on all the mysteries. But if there happened to be one really good reader or speaker, then he or she could do them all. Those conducting the vigil should be open to the Holy Spirit, to the inspiration of the moment. *Then* the vigil will be truly alive.

Prepared Meditations

We recommend the prepared meditations below, inviting different persons to read different parts.

We begin with the Sorrowful Mysteries because they offer a fitting preparation for the opening Mass (usually in honor of the Sacred Heart) and for the entire experience of the all night vigil.

The Joyful Mysteries, said in the first hours of the first Saturday, recall not only the essential mystery of Incarnation, but also the recent visitations of Our Lady with her program to renew all things in Christ, to bring about the triumph of the Sacred Hearts for a true order of peace in the world.

Finally the Glorious Mysteries climax the vigil and offer a fitting preparation for the closing Benediction and the Mass of the Immaculate Heart.

These meditations can also be used for Holy Hours and to fulfill the first Saturday obligation to meditate on the mysteries of the Rosary (as was noted in the first chapter). If no vigil is possible in a church within traveling distance, why not invite neighbors and have a vigil at home...directing one's love to the nearest tabernacle where Jesus today is often locked away, truly a Prisoner of Love!

To Introduce the Rosary

It is warmly recommended that brief prayers to the Father be said to introduce each mystery beginning immediately after the Creed (*before* the Our Father for each mystery):

O Eternal Father, we praise and thank You for sending Your Only Son into the world to redeem us, and for sending Him through Mary that we might have both a Redeemer and a Mother. By these mysteries we beg You to increase in us faith, hope, and love!

The following prayers can be used to "announce" each mystery:

Joyful Mysteries

1 - Dear Father, thank You for sending Your angel to ask Our Lady to become the Mother of Your Son and, at that same moment, our own Mother. Help us to understand this great mystery of Your Love!

2 - Dear Father, urged by the words of Your angel that *nothing is impossible to You,* Our Lady hastened to Her cousin Elizabeth. Grant, Father, that we, too, may live in the realization that to You nothing is impossible; that we, like St. John the Baptist, may be sanctified at the sound of Our Lady's greeting.

3 - Dear Father, Your Provident Power moved the head of the great Roman Empire to issue an edict to fulfill Your Will that Jesus be born in Bethlehem as foretold and You sent a miraculous star to lead kings from wafar. Lead us, O loving Father, and all the nations of the world, to Him, Who came to us in a manger to reveal to us that You are Love.

4 - Dear Father, as Your daughter Mary and Her spouse St. Joseph presented Your Incarnate Word in the temple, You sent Your Holy Spirit upon Simeon and Anna to recognize Him, and to see into Mary's Immaculate Heart. Grant us the light of that same Holy Spirit.

5 - Dear Father, You willed that Your daughter Mary and Her spouse St. Joseph should endure the trial of separation from Jesus, and the joy of having Him return to Nazareth to abide with them. Grant that we may endure the trial and have Jesus abide with us.

Sorrowful Mysteries

1 - Dear Father, in His agony in the garden Jesus cried out: "Not My Will but Thine be done!" O good Father, that I may ever accomplish Your Holy Will! Thy kingdom come! Thy Will be done!

2 - Father, we are appalled to see Your Divine Son bound and scourged, as He is "bound" in our tabernacle as a Prisoner of Love, scourged by our indifference and even by sacrilege. Grant, through the intercession of Our Lady, that we may console our Prisoner of Love!

3 - Father, they mocked the kingship of Your Divine Son with a crown of thorns. We affirm His kingship! May He reign in our lives! Thy Kingdom come!

4 - Father, we believe that Calvary is present at every Mass. To assist well at our next Mass we wish to follow in the footsteps of the Sorrowful and Immaculate Heart of Mary on the road to Calvary where, by His death, Jesus showed us that You are Love.

5 - The night before He died He said: "When you see Me, you see the Father." Dying He said: "Into Your Hands I commit My Spirit." O good Father, in the passion of Jesus may we recognize the greatness of Your love and mercy. By the intercession of the sorrowful and Immaculate Heart of Mary may many souls be saved by this prayer and that You be honored and loved in all the world!

Glorious Mysteries

1 - Dear Father, the first recorded words of Our dear Lord after His resurrection were: "Do not touch Me, I have not yet ascended to My Father!" He reminded us, as He had the night before He died, that He was sent by You to show us Your Love. Confirm us in the hope of our own resurrection to be with You forever.

2 - Ascending to You, dear Father, He said that You would send the Holy Spirit to make all things known to us, and He left His Mother behind to gather with the church in prayer, as we do now. Send Your Holy Spirit upon us and upon the Church!

3 - Father, You kept the promise Jesus made as He ascended to You, You sent the Holy Spirit with light and strength. Grant, beloved Father, through the intercession of Our Lady, His spouse, that we may receive His gifts.

4 - With what joy, Father, You received Your daughter Mary assumed into Heaven! We are told that, in this joy, all Purgatory was emptied. By Her intercession, grant relief to the Holy Souls and final contrition to all the dying! And grant that we may obtain, by Her motherly intercession, to be with You and the saints forever in Heaven.

5 - Eternal Father, we rejoice to live in this age of mercy when You have entrusted the peace of the world to Mary, our loving Mother! We hail Her as our Queen. See us clothed in Her livery and use us in Her service for the triumph of Your Kingdom in our nation and in all the nations of the world!

The Meditations

First Sorrowful Mystery

The Chosen Three

Why did Our Lord choose just three of the apostles to go aside with Him to suffer the night before He died?

Why did He choose the three who had seen Him transfigured on Tabor, and who were therefore most aware that He was God?

And did Our Lord not know that these three men would be asleep during the hour? Then what was the sense of inviting them to be with Him at all?

Like many of the mysteries of the Rosary, this is a mystery intended not so much for the moment when it happened as for all those subsequent moments in history when Christians finally would understand the meaning of what Our Lord did, and would apply the mystery to their own lives—*as we have done tonight in coming to be here, in this church, to be with Him.*

Just a couple of hours before His agony, Christ had instituted the Blessed Sacrament. He had given the world the greatest testament of His Love. *He had revealed the mystery of the Trinity. He had prayed that all men might be one as He and His Father were One.* At the peak of this revelation, one of the apostles who had been with Him for three whole years of His teachings, suddenly said: "Show us the Father, and then we will believe." Almost in exasperation the loving Master exclaimed in return: "Philip, *have I been with you so long and you do not know that when you see Me, you see the Father also?*"

We do not know why it was Peter, James, and John whom He invited aside with Him as went into the Garden to pray. He knew that before this very night was over, Peter would deny Him, and that even James, with the others, would flee. He could have endured the agony alone. He could have anticipated His Passion alone. Indeed, in the end, this is what He had to do. But He chose three to be with Him. And He has chosen us tonight.

He did not want to be alone.

He even came and woke them up, even though He knew that though they were willing in spirit they were just too tired to stay awake, and He lamented to them: *"Could you not watch one hour with Me?"*

Now, we are the chosen ones. We are here tonight— chosen by a mysterious call which we ourselves cannot quite define. Certainly there were many temptations to stay away. And perhaps five times as many as the number who are here received the call—but ultimately we remain *"the chosen ones."*

Those three apostles whom Our Lord took with Him fell asleep.

But He knew that 2000 years later there would be this night, and that others whom He would draw aside, finally, in the perspective of history, would be able to understand His lament: *"Could you not watch one hour with Me?"*—and in a burst of heroic love would say: *"Not one hour, dear Lord, but the night!"*

Even so, the spirit is willing but the flesh may be weak. During the course of the night our attention may wander. We may even be tempted to leave, to give up.

But we know much that Peter, James, and John did not know. *We know how much Christ wants us with Him.* We know He is truly present here in our midst...body, blood, soul and divinity; that He has come forth from that monstrance in that Host to Saint Margaret Mary with His Heart flaming with love to appeal for our presence here. Furthermore He sent His Mother to Fatima to tell us that the cause of wars in the world, the cause of the spread of atheistic communism, can be rooted out only in one way: by prayer and sacrifice.

For that reason Our Lady came at Fatima to plead with us for sacrifices like this night.

Showing us a vision of hell, She said: "*So many souls are lost because there is no one to pray and to make sacrifice for them.*" She appealed to all of us, at least to us who understand, to step aside from our daily lives, from the chores and the routine of our daily lives, to pray, to make sacrifice, to repair for the sins of the world.

That is why we are here tonight.

We hear not only the plea of Christ in the Garden two thousand years ago, but we hear the plea of Our Lady on a mountain today: "So many souls are lost because there is no one to pray and to make sacrifice for them."

So now, in these ten Hail Marys, as we witness the agony of Christ in the modern world mirrored in the numberless sins taking place tonight in this city (area) and throughout the world, we plead to Our Lady to help us with this hour of prayer and sacrifice.

With each Hail Mary we remind Her of Her divine Motherhood, we remind Her that we are poor sinners in need of Her prayers, and we plead with Her *to lend us Her Immaculate Heart for just this one hour* so that we may, in the most perfect way, respond to the thought that out of all the thousands of persons in this area, *we few are chosen to be here, because we want to console our Savior* and make reparations for our sins and those of our neighbors. (Optional—decade prayer to the Father, p. 38).

✝✝✝

Second Sorrowful Mystery

Blood On The Steps

The apostles in the Garden could not stay awake, yet Our Lord was no less human than they, and He had a far busier and more difficult day. Then while they slept, He went through the exhausting agony that was so terrible that it caused blood to ooze from His pores with perspiration.

While they could not watch one hour with Him, He was to spend his entire night in agony...yes, not only the entire night, *but all the rest of the day until He was to die in agony!*

After the first agony and the kiss of Judas, Our Lord was dragged to Annas and Caiaphas. He admitted that He claimed to be God and the high priest sentenced Him to death. But He still was not given over to sleep. He was turned over to the soldiers, who made sport of Him and finally tied a rope under His armpits and lowered Him into the security prison across the court from Pilate's house.

After Mary's womb, this prison became the world's first tabernacle. It is only a good stone's throw from the very room where Our Lord instituted the Blessed Sacrament, and here in prayer Our Lord spent the last minutes of that terrible night before again He was pulled forth and dragged down Mount Zion, around the temple and into the courtyard of the Fortress Antonia, where the emissaries of the high priest called upon Pilate to ratify their judgment and sign the order of execution.

Some of us were tempted not to make this hour of prayer and reparation. Some may have thought of coming just for the Mass, and of going back later to their comfortable beds. But now with what joy we anticipate spending this night with Our Lord *in memory of that night which He spent not in a comfortable church, in the presence of those He loved, but in hostile hands and destined for the worst torture man has ever known, culminating in the worst death man could conceive.*

Was it not enough that He had already endured the agony of the Garden and that He must endure the agony of the Cross? Was it not enough that He had already spent the entire night in prayer and sacrifice?

No, His love was too great to permit the word "enough." He willed to endure so much suffering that no one, in any age, could ever say that man had known or even imagined a greater love. He was to give *not only His night, not only His life, but His utmost limit of suffering.*

So we hear the terrible judgment of Pilate: *"Scourge Him."*

Many men have died under the scourging. Pilate thought that it would be the limit of suffering which might deter His persecutors from wanting to crucify a just man.

So badly torn was the sensitive body of this perfect Man that more than an hour after scourging, when Pilate still found that he could not escape the pressure of the mob and condemned Him to take the cross, *Blood dripped down His garments onto the steps* as He walked from the balcony of the Fortress down to the courtyard where the cross was waiting.

Christians of the first century marveled that those drops of Blood spilled upon the steps of the Fortress *had permeated the stone* and did not wash or wear away. When St. Helena came to the Holy Land in search of the holy places, just a few generations later, she found that Christians in the Holy City had all but forgotten where the Cross had been hidden, but were revering those twenty-eight steps of the Fortress Antonia where the drops of Blood were still to be seen.

So Helena had those great blocks of stone taken one by one, loaded on a ship, and brought to Rome where she built a special church just across from the Lateran Palace which had been given to the Pope as the first public center of the Catholic Church.

To this day we can see the Blood on the steps.

Why would Our Lord want me so vividly to remember this bloodshed other than that *He would want me to be here tonight* so that this Blood of the scourging will not have been shed in vain?

Is this not, too, why Our Lady came at Fatima showing Her Sorrowful and Immaculate Heart? Is this is not why She pleaded with me: "So many Souls are lost because there is no one to pray and make sacrifice for them?"

Most of the world has forgotten the Blood on the steps. Most of the world has forgotten the Passion of Christ and the meaning of suffering in the world. Most of the world has forgotten that souls are falling into hell "like leaves from the trees in autumn," as St. Theresa said, because there is no one to pray and to make sacrifices that they may have the grace of final contrition.

I now turn to Our Lady in these ten Hail Marys and plead with Her to. give me the understanding of the terrible Passion of Christ, the Christ in whose presence I kneel at this moment and the flame of whose love I feel searing my heart.

I ask Her in these ten Hail Marys *to please lend me Her own Immaculate Heart that I may worthily spend this night in union with the night of Christ's Passion* and may fulfill the special calling of being one of the few taken aside from the world to participate in this hour of love. (Optional—decade prayer to the Father, p. 38).

Third Sorrowful Mystery

The Thorns

Pilate was not joking when he said to Our Lord: "Are You a king?"

There was something regal about Christ, and Pilate, a man of authority, recognized it.

The soldiers to whom Pilate had given Christ for scourging also recognized this regality, this kingliness. It disturbed them. The only way they knew how to tolerate it was to mock it.

They blindfolded Him so that they could not look into those regal eyes, and then they put a purple rag around His shoulders, a reed in His hands for a scepter and thrust a cruel crown of thorns upon His head.

This crown of thorns has become one of the most important symbols of the Passion of Christ. It symbolizes the mockery of His Kingship.

Is that why Our Lady, when she appeared at Fatima, showed the crown of thorns around her Immaculate Heart?

The most widespread, and in a sense the most terrible sin of our time, is the mockery and neglect of Christ, our King. Not so much by those who do not know and do not believe, but by those who should know and should believe. That is the main reason we are here tonight. We are here to make reparation for all those who are not here.

We are here to make reparation for all those who pass by Our Lord truly present in churches in almost every city and town around the world. We are here to make reparation for those who live their entire lives without once turning their heads to acknowledge His authority.

For what greater sin could be committed against a person of authority than to be ignored?

When we watch a television program and see people dying before our eyes in these dramas, how often do we hear them invoke the name of God? As we see all the world bustling around us, how often do we see it bending its knee to its Creator? Is this not truly the great sin of our time, the sin of the crown of thorns, the sin of mockery?

A minister released from a Communist prison in Rumania said that the greatest torture endured by Christians in the camp was not the physical torture as much as the mockery. He described how four Christians were tied to crosses in a compound of over a hundred prisoners, and other prisoners half mad with hunger and suffering were forced to void themselves upon the faces and bodies of those tied to the crosses. Then the crosses were raised and all in the prison were told, "There is your Christ, adore Him! He brings you fragrances from heaven!"

He told of even far more terrible things which we fear to mention, and that there were things yet more terrible which he himself did not have the courage to repeat.

This kind of mockery we can understand. It is the mockery of those who know, and who hate.

But what about *the mockery of those who know and who don't care?* If the Holy Father, or the President of the United States, or our bishop were standing in front of this church looking out upon you, ready to have each of you come up and shake his hand, what an affront it would be if each person got up and simply turned and walked passed him without a nod!

Yet daily this kind of affrontery is offered to Christ in churches, in towns, in cities, in every part of the world.

Will this night be long enough for us to make reparation? How few we are who have come to tell Our Lord that we love Him, that we recognize His Kingship, that we want to lift away the crown of thorns and place upon Him instead, the true crown of the King of Kings, *a crown which only our love can fashion.*

Certainly we are not worthy to be here. Certainly we have not a love great enough to fashion this crown for our King. So we turn now with all the fervor of our hearts to our Mother, who came to Fatima with Her Immaculate Heart surrounded by the crown of thorns. We plead with Her these ten Hail Marys to send us Her Immaculate Heart that with it we may reach such a state of love in the course of this night that for at least this brief moment, Our Lord may receive the crown of love His own love deserves. (Optional—decade prayer to the Father, p. 38).

Fourth Sorrowful Mystery

The Carrying of the Cross

Our Lord carried the cross from the Fortress Antonia in front of the great Temple, across the entire city of Jerusalem.

About half the distance was downhill from the Fortress and the rest was up. He carried the beam, despite His entire night without sleep and all the tortures to which He had been subjected, all the way from the Fortress to the low point of the journey, almost half way to Calvary. There He fell as He turned a corner, and there Our Lady saw Him.

He left His dear mother in Bethany with St. John. He needed Her, but certainly He did not want Her to witness His Passion. But She had come into the city through another way, and She was approaching the street down which He was carrying the beam when suddenly He turned the corner and She saw Him fall there.

The crowd was so dense that She could not get closer. But about twenty yards from where He fell, He passed so closely that She could almost have embraced Him, were it not for the soldiers.

How can we imagine the emotion that filled the heart of Mary as She saw Her Divine Son, thirty-three years of age, His face disfigured with the Blood from the crown of thorns, His cloak stained through with the Blood of the scourging, His whole weakened body bent under the weight of the beam, and the street filled with the noises and abuse, and the hatred of His enemies?

We won't try to imagine the love and sympathy which filled the heart of this purest and most loving of all mothers. We cannot.

But at least we can vaguely understand *why She has come so urgently in our own times, again and again, to plead with us for prayer for the conversion of sinners.* We can understand why She has obtained from God, in our own time, a miracle on the mountain of Fatima at a predicted time and place so that the whole world might believe and *there might be at least a few who would come to spend a night like this in reparation and sacrifice,* in prayer for the conversion of sinners, that the suffering witnessed that day in that street would not have been in vain.

Let us notice something else.

From this moment there was a radical change in Our Lord's Passion. It would seem that He was bent upon enduring everything possible, with no alleviation whatever.

But from the moment His eyes met the eyes of His mother, three things happened in rapid succession. First, the soldiers took the beam from His shoulders and placed it upon those of a farmer; next a woman came forth to wipe His blood-stained face; and then a whole group were found weeping for Him just before He stumbled and fell through the gate in the very shadow of the rock upon which He would die. It would seem as if His mother, who obtained from Him at Cana a miracle before His time had come, in that one glance on the Via Dolorosa, obtained from Him and the Father alleviation of His Passion.

So now I turn to my Mother in these next ten Hail Marys and plead with Her to make me another Simon of Cyrene, and to give us more persons like those here at this vigil, persons willing to take the cross from the shoulders of Christ and make reparation for sinners. I plead with Her in these ten Hail Marys to help me, at least during this night, to be another Veronica. With each passing moment of these night hours I offer to Christ the towel of my love, asking Him to impress upon it the Image of Himself, not that I may be rewarded for being here, but that I may never forget the loving exchange that takes place between my heart and His Heart during this sacred night.

Finally I ask Her to give me the tears of compassion, and to understand His admiration that I weep not just for the suffering that I witness, but that I weep for the sins that cause it. I ask Her to give me the true sense of repentance for my own sins, a true sense of horror for the evil of sin, and to lend me Her Immaculate Heart that I may, at least during this night, make reparation to my Jesus, my Savior, my Love. (Optional—decade prayer to the Father, p. 38).

Fifth Sorrowful Mystery

The Crucifixion

What would it have been like to have been at the foot of the Cross when Our Lord died?

Have I ever envied John, or Mary Magdalen, or even the good thief, or even the Roman soldier who thrust the lance into Our Lord's dead body and who was forced to exclaim: "Indeed this was the Son of God!"?

Well, in a few moments, I will actually be present at Calvary. This is what the Sacrifice of the Mass means in its deepest sense. In just a few moments I will be participating in the Mass of the Sacred Heart.

To God all things and all points of time are continually present. All events of history are to Him like a long parade seen from a high place. Someone watching a parade from street level can see only the small part of the parade directly in front and to the right and left of him. But a person on a very high building can look down and see perhaps the beginning and the end of the parade, as well as what is passing directly below. The events of history, in time, are like this to God.

So when the priest says on the altar, "This is My Body," and then over the wine says, "This is My Blood," it is as though I, too, were suddenly spirited to a very high place and were able to see that I am present at Calvary.

But what a poor comparison! Because I am not spirited away at all. *Calvary is brought here to me!* Have I ever truly understood the Mass in this way? Or have I only looked upon the Mass as the means by which Christ comes in our midst? Our Lord said: "If I be lifted above the ground, I will draw all things to Myself."

The Evangelist tells us that by this He meant the manner in which He would die, and that through this terrible death of crucifixion, through hours of culminating agony after the world's first all-night vigil, the gates of heaven would be open for all time. Souls in Limbo would suddenly see God for the first time after centuries of privation. The forces of Satan would be greatly diminished, and ultimately there would come a day when enough people would make reparation for others. Graces, obtained by vigils like this, would flow upon the world, opening the eyes of many in darkness to the spiritual Truth which alone can make possible the great peace and unity of all men, even as Christ Himself is One with the Father. Not this night, nor all the nights of my life, nor all the waking minutes of my life would be enough to understand this mystery.

From the moment I hear the sound of the hammer upon the nails; from the moment I see Our Lord stretched upon the cross and see His every muscle tensed to take the weight from His chest that He may live those hours of His seven last words; surely through the sympathetic agony of Mary, the anguish of John, the grief of Magdalen, the sudden awesome faith of the dying thief, I must realize above all that this is a sacrifice for me, me, me. *I have been told that if I were the only human being in the world, Our Lord would have done this for me.*

Now, in a few moments in this very church, through the Sacrifice of the Mass, I am going to be present there, really and truly. I can speak to Our Lord during the moment of consecration and in the minutes that follow, exactly as I would have spoken to Him were I in the place of the thief, in the place of John, or—O heavenly thought—in the place of His own Blessed Mother.

I have come here tonight to make reparation because Our Lord came out of the monstrance in a chapel in France and told St. Margaret Mary that there were so few to love Him in the Sacrament of His Love. He pleaded with her for hours of reparation before Him, especially on this very night. But in those days, an evening Mass was not permitted.

Now I am living in a time when I can be present at Calvary tonight to honor Our Lord's Sacred Heart for the first Friday, and then I can climax my all night vigil by being present again at Calvary, in union with the Immaculate Heart of Mary, only a few hours later. How fortunate I am to live in this time, when during this single night of reparation I can have the opportunity of being twice present at Calvary! For if I am to make reparation for sin, how better can I do it than sharing with the Immaculate Heart of Mary at the foot of the Cross?

A holy man once said that if we had but one drop of the love that filled the heart of Mary as She stood at the foot of the Cross, we would be lost in an ocean of love. Therefore, dearest Mother, reminding You that it is because of Your appeal to me at Fatima that I have come here tonight, I plead with You to lend me Your Immaculate Heart. St. Grignon says that You have the key to the cellar of Divine Love.

Open those doors, dearest Mother, to so transform my heart with love that, as I am about to assist at this Holy Mass, Our Lord may behold not me, but You—His loving Mother—and hear only Your words as I say to Him that I desire the conversion of sinners. I desire that the Blood that He has shed upon Calvary shall not have been shed in vain, and that soon there may be such an unleashing of grace and love upon the world, that bigotry, and ignorance, and hatred, and sinfulness that seems to surround us will be swept away in that ocean of grace. (Optional—decade prayer to the Father, p. 38).

First Joyful Mystery

An Angel Speaks

As I find myself here in this church looking at that piece of white matter in the monstrance on the altar perhaps my greatest difficulty, my greatest obstacle to realization that this white disc is Christ, living, complete, Body, Blood, Soul, and Divinity, is not so much that I have difficulty believing that God could perform such a stupendous miracle, could change bread into Himself. My greater obstacle is to accepting the fact that God could love me this much.

Can God, Who is Infinite, Who has created the world, Who holds all things in His hands, love me so much that He wanted to be a prisoner, to be transubstantiated with common food stuff, so that He could be united to me as intimately as food itself, and as present to me as He is this moment before my eyes?

Certainly the God Who created the world *could* do this. Certainly the God Who made my body, with all its complicated mechanisms, its eyes, its sensitiveness, its ability to coordinate hearing, touch, and sight into a single thought, certainly this God **could make Himself present before me** in any form He chose.

But how could He love me this much?

This is the greatest of all mysteries which has been chanted down the centuries in the words of the psalmist: "What is man, O Lord, that Thou art mindful of Him?"

Could such a thought have crossed the mind of Mary when She heard the words of the Angel, "Hail Mary, full of grace, the Lord is with Thee?" Could such a thought have crossed the mind of Mary when She protested that She was not worthy, was not in the position to become the instrument of the Incarnation?

No, because Our Lady knew the greatness of God's love.

Therefore, when She was certain She had been chosen She was able, without a single moment of hesitation, to say to the angel: **"Be it done unto me according to Thy word."**

And at that moment, for the first time, God became physically present on earth. God united Himself with matter. Mary became the world's first tabernacle.

Where am I going to get the understanding that will enable me to see that there is no greater mystery in the Host before me than in that speck in Mary's womb that was God? Where am I going to get the faith to understand that God, Infinite Creator though He be, loves me and loves me so much that He not only became man, but then transubstantiated Himself with bread so that in the fullness of His humanity and divinity, He could be present to me in churches everywhere?

This very night He called me aside, He gave me the special grace to be here in His presence. He has called me, in a sense, to be another Mary.

I am not worthy of this privilege. How many temptations assailed me before I decided to come here for this night! How many times in the past I made excuses! With how many sins upon my soul do I find myself in His presence?

Oh, yes, in His great mercy my sins have been forgiven because I have confessed them and have resolved to try not to commit them again. But they are there. I see the monstrous accumulation of their scars. I wonder how He can stand me in His sight; I, who have betrayed Him so often; I, who think so much of myself; I, who am so sensitive to the good opinion of others, so ready to bury myself in the pleasures of the world around me, so ready rather to spend wasteful hours before a television set than precious minutes before Him.

Yes, I will turn to Mary, my Mother. She knows how much God loves me. She can obtain for me the grace to understand.

Certainly, when I understand, I will want to return that love. I will want these moments before Jesus, truly present as man and God, to go on and on and on. *This night will never be long enough to say how much I wish to return His love* and how much more and more and more I want to understand His relationship to me.

Oh, already I feel an understanding—not of why He loves me, because that I could never understand—but that He does love me. He loves me not only enough to unite Himself with my nature, but He loves me enough to endure all the Passion, and then to transubstantiate Himself with bread to show the extent and depth of His infinite love.

What return shall I make to Him? Well, in my own day, His Mother told me how. She has appeared repeatedly, lamenting with tears the lack of love in the world and said that it is only because of this that terrible wars afflict us, that militant atheism was spreading to the whole world, and that only when men would respond to the neglected love of Christ in the tabernacle, would the atheists be converted and would the world find peace.

So in these next ten Hail Marys, dearest Mother, I turn to you not just for an understanding of the love that caused God to become man, and caused Him to be present here before me now, even as at the moment of Incarnation He became present in You. But I ask You above all, to give me the light and the grace to return this great love.

God, Who is all good and Who is my Creator, has given Himself to me. Won't you pray dearest Mother, that I may know how to give my soiled self to Him? Just for this night *lend me Your Immaculate Heart. Lend me the fire of Your love, the depth of Your faith, the height of Your hopes, and the strength of Your heart to plead successfully for the conversion of a thousand sinners who otherwise would be lost.*

Let Your Immaculate Heart take the place of my heart, so that just for these passing minutes at least He may find a worthy return of love, and all mankind may be lifted closer to the realization of the great promise You made at Fatima. If enough of Your children would pray in this way, You promised that the world would find unity and peace.

In a word, dearest Mother, somehow let me take Your place in the house in Nazareth as I now repeat the words the Angel spoke to You, so that once again God may intimately enter our world. (Optional—decade prayer to the Father, p. 38).

†††

Second Joyful Mystery

Unborn Child

Have you ever wondered why God chose to come to the world in the way He did, nine months in Mary's womb and then born in a stable?

Would it have required a greater miracle for Christ to have appeared as a man of thirty, full of wisdom and knowledge, no one knowing from whence He had come? Would He have not been accepted much more readily had He come as a full-grown man? Was not the greatest stumbling block for the Jews the fact that they could say over and over again: "Is this not the son of Joseph the carpenter? Is this man not from Nazareth?"

There may be many reasons why God chose to become man by first becoming a tiny, almost invisible speck in the womb of Mary. But certainly one of the greatest of these reasons is that He was to emphasize the tremendous dignity of parenthood.

Is there any dignity possible to men, outside of the other Sacraments, than the dignity of parenthood, the exalted power and right to bring new human life into the world, to be a procreator with God? Oh, how many sin against this tremendous dignity! How many times during my own life I have sinned against it!

As I see Our Lady now taking the arduous journey from Nazareth to Ein Karim, a journey of several days, I marvel at the mystery of God having become man and dwelling in Her all-pure womb. I marvel at Mary becoming the world's first Christopher, bearing Christ from the very moment that He has come forth to the world, forth to a new mystery, the mystery of Her cousin who has been childless for years and now beyond the years of childbearing has been miraculously blessed.

As Our Lady finally comes to the house of Elizabeth, the saintly cousin is struck with faith and cries out, "Whence is it that the Mother of my Lord should come to me?" At that moment she felt the six-month infant in her womb leap with joy, and in that moment, Christ performed His first miracle: the miracle of the pre-sanctification of St. John in the womb of Elizabeth.

Once again I witness the emphasis that God gives from the first moment of His coming into the world to the dignity of parenthood. I marvel that the very first miracle of Christ, as Mary bore Him on His first journey in the world, should be the presanctification of an unborn child. And I think of all the sins of abortion, all the sins for the prevention of the birth of children that are taking place this very night, all over this globe.

I myself have been guilty of these or similar sins. It is my brothers, my fellow men, who are committing these sins now, at this very moment, outrages upon the greatest dignity of man.

Why am I here tonight in the presence of the same Christ Whom Mary bore to Elizabeth?

I am here to make reparation. I am here to repair the offenses against this great dignity of man. I am here to tell Our Lord that I deplore the flaunting, and the degrading, and the abuse of this dignity which fills my world at this moment. I can't wipe it all away. I can't snatch all the improper books and magazines from the stands. I cannot close the theaters that are showing improper pictures. I cannot enter the homes and argue with thousands of individuals who don't understand or who don't care to understand. But I can kneel here before Him as one member of the human race and, enclosed with the faith, love, and trust of Mary, I can try to make up in some small measure for the sins around me.

St. Alphonsus asked: "Why did Elizabeth say, 'Whence is it that the Mother of my Lord should come to me?' Why didn't she say: 'Whence is it that the Incarnate God has come to me?'" St. Alphonsus answers his own question by saying that Elizabeth knew that in welcoming the Mother she was welcoming the Son.

This, too, I vaguely understand as I choose to say this decade of the Rosary in the presence of the Incarnate God. I know that in finding Mary I find Him, and that in addressing Mary I am reaching His heart with the greatness of Her love. I know that somehow He will no longer see my unworthiness, my accumulation of neglect and wrong doing, but rather will behold my desire to use only Her Immaculate Heart to love Him now at this moment, to make reparation.

Therefore, dearest Mother, as I see You hastening along the road and coming to the house of Elizabeth, bearing the Incarnate God, I plead with You in these next ten Hail Marys to give me the love that I need at this moment to repair for the sins around me, and for all my own sins in the past, as Our Lord intended I should, when He chose to bring me here tonight. (Optional—decade prayer to the Father, p. 38).

ttt

Third Joyful Mystery

Disappearing Star

The three kings, who had the special privilege of being chosen out of all the world to be led to Bethlehem on the night Christ was born, had to travel a great distance. Some of us here in the presence of Christ now, also have had to come from a distance. But no matter from where we have come, we had to arrange things at home, we had to arrange transportation, we had to organize our time. This alone was the first great step. Even were I not to complete this night as gloriously full of faith and as wide awake and energetic as I would want to be, I thank Our Lord for the grace first, of having been called to be here, and secondly, for the strength to overcome the many temptations that would have prevented my answering that call.

What was the star that led me? Someone who participated in many all night vigils and holy hours made it a point to inquire of different ones what devotions in their lives might have given them the grace to participate in such a holy exercise, and he found that in every instance the persons who were there had a very special devotion to the Blessed Virgin, and almost all of them had the practice of saying the daily Rosary!

So Mary, even though I may not have known it, is my Star. She is the Star that God has set into the darkness of the human night, so that even when men are lost in the darkness of sin they can look up, they can know that the night will pass, they can find a guidance that will see them through until the dawn.

It is not mere tradition that the three kings came from the area of Persia, which would mean that they had to travel about a thousand miles. When St. Helena came to the Holy Land in the early part of the fourth century, the Basilica that she built over the place of the birth of Our Lord was filled with Persian inscriptions to honor the kings; and in the seventh century when the Persians invaded the Holy Land, this was the only church that they did not destroy— because of the Persian symbols honoring the kings who had followed the star to the birth of Christ.

Along their journey how many times these good men must have been tempted to turn back! Could they ever have foreseen that their journey would be so long? Even before they set out, were they not tempted in many ways to avoid this unknown journey?

But certainly they became a comfort one to another. When one might be discouraged, then perhaps at that moment another might have the right word to say. Could this not be the reason why God chose three men to come from a distance and to follow the star together?

How many of us would be here tonight if it were not for some friend who called us on the telephone, who dropped us a note, who offered to come with us? If other travelers are to follow this road to find Jesus, then I, too, must have the fortitude and the charity to help. For together at the end of our road we shall appear before Christ in the Eucharist and have the great joy that must have filled the hearts of the kings when, as scripture summarizes the climax of their journey, "entering in they found the Child with Mary, His Mother."

Yes, I have believed before in the true presence of Our Lord in the Eucharist. I often have knelt in His presence. But tonight I feel a special love, a special faith. Tonight as I pray this Rosary and ask Our Lady to make me a repairer of the sins of the world around me as of my own sins in the past, I feel a new depth of understanding of the presence of Christ. I feel a new appreciation of the love of God that caused Him to take this form to unite Himself to me, to be present to me. With every passing minute of this vigil I somehow feel ever more deeply the joy of those kings: "Finding the Child with Mary, His Mother."

Dearest Mother, I do not envy the shepherds who were summoned by the song of an angel to the cave in Bethlehem. I do not even envy Joseph who stood beside You. I do not envy the kings who had this star to lead them that night and who were the first of the Gentiles to know of the Incarnation. For this very day not only have I knelt here in His presence, beholding Him with new eyes of faith, experiencing in a special way the depth of His love, but I have the enormous grace of Communion, the grace of being present at Calvary, the grace of communing with Him as intimately as did the apostles at the Last Supper. Oh, what return shall I make for the great grace that is mine?

Sometimes, dearest Mother, the star goes out, as it did for the kings when they arrived at Jerusalem. Sometimes I feel nothing. But I know that I do not need tangible feeling to carry me on. I can reason. I can ask. My faith tells me that even though I don't feel or see, I have been truly called, and that the desire of my heart to be with God came truly from Him, and therefore cannot be false. It will lead me to Him.

Whether or not the star shines for me at this moment, I ask You in these next ten Hail Marys to give this moment to Him...and all the moments of my life, as You were pleased to accept the incense, the gold and the myrrh

The gold I offer is my faith, even when the star doesn't shine. The incense I offer is my trust in the mercy of God, even though I cannot see the star shining. The myrrh I offer is my love.

I ask You in these next ten Hail Marys to be my Mother in a special way. Be my Star. Even when I cannot feel You near me, but especially at this moment when I kneel in the divine presence of Your Son, fill me with the sentiments that filled the hearts of You and St. Joseph on that holy night, that I may repair for the thoughtlessness of the world around me, as Your love repaired for the thoughtlessness of the town of Bethlehem.

Our Lady was not bound by the law of purification. Why then did She and St. Joseph make the long trip from Nazareth to Jerusalem? Was it just because of human respect? No, this could not be, because they could have set out on the road and no one ever would have known whether or not they had come to Jerusalem.

Another question: Why did they not go merely to the local synagogue rather than going all the way into Jerusalem?

As in all the great mysteries of the Rosary (the mysteries of the life of Christ) there are many reasons, there are many depths to explore. But one mystery here is particularly challenging to me as I am spending this vigil here in the presence of my Eucharistic Christ.

There was a man in that Temple who had a daring faith. Indeed, in all the annals of history we would have difficulty in finding a man of greater daring.

While his ancestors before him, and millions of his contemporaries, prayed merely for the coming of the

Messiah, this man dared to pray that he would live to see the Messiah in his own lifetime! He did not pray as others did that the Savior of the world would come soon, or one day. He dared to pray consistently, day after day, month after month, year after year, that the Savior of the world would come now.

An old man, weighted by many years of service in the Temple, still he prayed as he had always: "Lord, that I may live to see the Savior of the world!"

Oh, wonder of wonders! Mary and Joseph, carrying the child, made the long journey to Jerusalem and came that day into the Temple. Many around in the corridors and passages of the great Temple saw only a young couple bringing a child for purification, even as many around us in this very city see only a white Host in the box before us. But the holy Simeon, the man of faith, beheld much more. There in that babe in the arms of Mary and Joseph he beheld the answer to his prayers, the Savior of the world! Going forth he took the Child from Mary's arms and raising his eyes to heaven broke forth in that magnificent canticle: "Now, O Lord, dismiss your servant in peace. My eyes have beheld the salvation of the world."

What a glorious fulfillment of prayer!

What was my intention in coming here tonight, coming here where I, too, can take the Child from Mary's arms, where by Holy Communion I can be more deeply united to Him even than Simeon could experience; and where I can kneel before Him and gaze upon Him and bathe myself in His love? How great is the daring of my prayer in these precious moments?

Am I praying for a child, a relative, a friend? Am I praying for some material want? Oh, what small things these are! Didn't Our Lord tell me: "All these things will be added to you!"?

Our Lady has come to our world a number of times, recently at Fatima, Akita, and other places, to ask me to pray for something else. At each one of Her comings, She asked over and over this very same thing. She asked me to pray for the conversion of sinners.

How much have I prayed for them? How many sinners have I saved by my sacrifice and prayer? How many do I hope to save by this vigil tonight? Am

I praying just that "some souls" will be saved? Am I praying just that the world may be "better?"

Let me pause for a moment and consider just how daring my prayer might be.

What do I feel would do most in my city to help sinners? For example, what about the theaters? What about the pornographic literature? What about the many public locations of sin? What about persons who are actually supporting laws for putting obstacles in my way of overcoming these locations of sin? Would I dare to pray for the absolute complete removal of such obstacles?

If I am going to pray for the individual conversion of sinners, which is perhaps the most practical and direct way to apply my daring, then for how many sinners might I dare to pray? Might I hope that this vigil might obtain enough grace to give final contrition to one sinner? To ten? To a hundred?

Saint Alphonsus Ligouri tells us of a Sister whom he knew who once dared to make a novena for the conversion of a thousand sinners. She prayed that before the end of her novena a thousand souls, who otherwise would have died in the state of mortal sin, would die in the state of Grace.

About half way through the novena Saint Alphonsus tells us that the good Sister realized that she was asking a great deal, so she decided to reduce the number to a fraction of one thousand. But hardly had she done so than Our Lady appeared to her, chided her for lack of faith, and said that already because of that novena a thousand souls, who otherwise would have been damned, had the grace of final contrition!

If one novena to Our Lady could obtain a thousand souls even before it was over, then why should I not dare to pray that just because of this vigil a thousand souls otherwise would have died tonight in the state of mortal sin, would be given the Grace of final contrition?

Is this too daring? Oh, yes, it would be too daring for me because I am not a Simeon. But would it be too daring for Our Lady?

Oh—if I had the Immaculate Heart of Mary with which to pray—if I had Her faith, Her hope, Her love—

then here in the presence of Our Lord I might dare to ask certainly even for more than a thousand sinners!

Why did Our Lady appear at Fatima and hold out Her Immaculate Heart? Why did She ask us to take the Scapular and be consecrated to Her in a special way, if it was not that She wanted us to clothe our hearts with Her heart? Indeed, why did God give us this Mother if it was not that we should find Him through Her?

As the Protestant poet Wordsworth said: "She is our tainted nature's solitary boast." If I cannot boast of my own goodness, certainly I can boast that this Mother is my Mother. I can beg Her in these next ten Hail Marys as I see Her going up to the Temple to give Her child to Simeon, the daring saint, to lend me Her heart for this night, that I, too, might have the daring to pray for that which She begged of me at Fatima: the conversion of sinners...many sinners. (Optional—decade prayer to the Father, p. 38).

†††

Fifth Joyful Mystery

In Her Heart

How can we think of the loss of Our Lord for three days as a Joyful Mystery?

It was joyful for many reasons. It was joyful because it is a mystery of the sorrow of loss turned into the joy of finding; it is joyful because Our Lord, even at this early age, was giving an intimation that He was going to live, not only in Palestine, but would one day be found in every church in the world, about His Father's business; it is joyful because, as St. John said when Jesus left Jerusalem with Mary and Joseph who went down to Nazareth to be "subject" to them for the next eighteen years, "Mary kept all these things, pondering them in Her Heart."

In our day, Our Lady came and revealed her Immaculate Heart at Fatima. It seems that now, more than ever, She wants to share with the world all the mysteries which She gathered up during the life of Our Lord, all the fullness of Grace that God has chosen to pour into this vessel of love, Her Immaculate Heart.

The heart is a symbol of love. That is why Our Lord chose this symbol when He came out of the Blessed Sacrament to St. Margaret Mary Alacoque and pleaded for reparation to Him in the Blessed Sacrament. He showed her a Heart flaming with love and said: "Behold the Heart which has so loved men."

So is it any wonder in our time, when the world has for too long ignored the Sacred Heart and plunged itself to the verge of atomic destruction, that Our Lady should offer Her Immaculate Heart, that as St. John Eudes said: "Children may have but one heart with their mother, and thus have a heart worthy of returning the love of the Heart of Christ"?

If I have not found Jesus so far in my life, is it not because I have been looking for Him all by myself?

Oh, of course I have found Him to some degree. Otherwise I would not be here for this night. But have I really found him? Does my heart burn within me as I kneel here before His Sacred Heart? Am I aware of Him every moment during the day, no matter where I am? Do my thoughts instinctively turn toward the nearest tabernacle where He is truly present? Do I know that He is to be found in the nearest church "about His Father's business," every moment of the day? Do I long constantly to be with Him?

No, I must admit that truly I have not found Him in the deepest and fullest sense. Therefore, it also must be true that I have not found Mary. I have not clothed my heart with Her Immaculate Heart. I have not brought the fire and purity and depth of faith which fills Her heart into mine.

Where shall I turn for help? How shall I place my heart into Her Immaculate Heart? How can I make the heart of my Mother my own?

First, I know that I have the devotion of the Scapular— the devotion Our Lady gave me so many centuries ago that has been so enriched with indulgences, the sign which She held in Her hands in the miracle of the sun in Her final appearance at Fatima. I know that this is a sign belonging to Her in a special way, and when my heart beats beneath this sign, then I know that it is beating close to Hers. Saint Claude, the great apostle of the Sacred Heart, said that while so many holy people through the centuries had longed to be near Mary, he had only to reach out and touch his hand upon the Scapular and he *knew* that Mary was near, he knew that his heart beat next to Hers, because that was implied in the great promise She made when She first gave the Scapular to the world.

Then I can turn to St. Joseph, who loved Mary more than any other man. Was he not chosen to be Her guardian? Was he not with Her through all the mysteries of Our Lord growing into manhood?

So I can turn to St. Joseph and ask him, as my own father and protector, to pray that I may come closer to Mary, that I may appreciate Her love, Her motherhood, and above all the purity and charity of Her heart so that I may love Her to such a degree that She will give Her heart to me to be mine.

Then there are all the saints of history, all who have been distinguished for the love of Our Lord in the Eucharist and for Mary.

A writer who was preparing a book on the Blessed Sacrament went to the biographies of as many saints as he could find. There were more than 300 volumes in all. And *in each and every one* he found a special chapter on *the saint's "extraordinary" devotion to Mary, and another chapter on the saint's "extraordinary" devotion to the Eucharist.*

In almost every book the distinguishing characteristics of each and every saint was a "special" or "extraordinary" devotion to Our Lady and the Eucharist to such an extent that they were seen to be the most important aspects of the saint's life.

So there is no canonized saint to whom I cannot cry out with confidence to obtain for me a great love for Mary so that I may borrow Her Immaculate Heart to come closer to the Sacred Heart of Our Lord in the Eucharist.

Let us pause now to think of the saints in whom we have greatest confidence. Let us repeat the prayer of each saint in our hearts, and when we say "Pray for us," let us intend that this saint will obtain for us a greater intimacy with the Immaculate Heart of Mary.

(A minute of silence may be made here, or we may mention one or more of these saints in particular: St. Theresa, St. Alphonsus, St. Margaret Mary, St. John Eudes, St. Peter Julian, St. Anna Marie Goretti, St. Francis, St. Anthony, St. Peter, St. Paul, St. James, St. John, St. Therese, St. Catherine Labouré, St. Bernadette, St. John Vianney, Blessed Anne Marie, St. Martin de Pores, St. Rose, St. Laurence, St. Pascal, St. Ignatius, St. Dominic, St. Simon, St. Catherine, St. John of the Cross, St. Paul of the Cross, St. Bernard, St. Louis Grignion de Montfort.)

Now, dearest Mother, fortified by the prayers of Your saints, I call upon You in these next ten Hail Marys, as I see You proceeding down to Nazareth with St. Joseph and the Child Jesus while contemplating all the mysteries of the Incarnation and His relation to man in Your Immaculate Heart. Please fill me with the awe of these mysteries, and to lend me Your Immaculate Heart with which to honor Him worthily as I kneel at this moment in His presence. (Optional—decade prayer to the Father, p. 38).

The Glorious Mysteries

The Whispered Name

Magdalen's eyes were dim with tears, her mind dulled by lack of sleep and grief, as she arrived at the tomb and found it empty. At that early morning hour, that man moving in the garden could be only the gardener. She cried out to him: "Sir, where have you taken Him?"

"Mary!" He replied. How often I have failed to *recognize* Our Lord in the Blessed Sacrament...

Oh, yes, I have it on faith that He is truly present, body, blood, soul, and divinity.

But how often have I heard Him whisper my name and really recognized Him? How often have my Communions, or my presence before Him as at this moment, been such that my heart reached to engulf His Heart, even as Mary ran to throw Herself upon Him?

In these next ten Hail Marys I am going to ask my Mother, to whom Our Lord most certainly came first at the very moment of His resurrection, *to cause His name to be so whispered in my heart during this vigil that I may recognize Him as did Magdalen, and that the meager fire of love in my heart may mingle with the flames of love in His.*

Again in this mystery I am reminded of the humanness of Christ, of His personal interest in me.

Three days before, at the Last Supper, while reclining at the table, John actually *rested his head on Our Lord's bosom. That was the first physical act of love and adoration to the Sacred Heart,* the prelude to St. John's first Communion.

Now again Magdalen threw herself upon Him, fondling Him so that He had to restrain her: "Do not touch Me. I have not yet ascended to My Father."

Usually Our Lord cured by touching people, or by being touched by them. He used physical things, even something as lowly as spittle mixed with dust, to place His Infinite Power in contact with us.

Now in His risen glory, bearing the lightsome scars of His Passion, He is present before me under the species of bread. I know this is so because He has told me. I know this is so because during 2,000 years, men of great intellect and wisdom have believed in this mystery and died for it. I know it because of the tremendous number of miracles He has performed in His Eucharistic state, possibly even more than He did in all of His life in Palestine.

But I want to hear Him whisper my name. I want to recognize Him as Magdalen did. I want the scales to fall from my eyes so that I can see Him with the eyes of faith so clearly that my heart will leap up within me, and the minutes of this vigil will be all too short to tell Him of my love, and to make reparation for all those who ignore Him in His Sacrament of Love.

Again after His resurrection, He appeared on the road and met two disciples who were journeying a distance from Jerusalem. They were sad and were discussing His crucifixion. He walked along with them, and even though they had known Him and heard Him preach, and had seen His miracles, *they did not recognize Him.* He was shrouded in the night, and had they not seen Him die? How could they have imagined that this stranger walking in the dark was He?

Then when they came to the inn, He pretended to be going on, and they had to beg Him to tarry with them. Finally came the great moment. He broke the bread and they recognized Him!

How often I have felt Our Lord walking with me, but I could not see Him clearly. My heart has burned with envy as I have heard words such as I am hearing now, or had thoughts such as I am having during this vigil. Yet I haven't seen Him clearly. I haven't heard Him speak my name. I earnestly desire this favor now, not for my own satisfaction, but so that I may more completely and worthily return the greatness of His love.

Dearest Mary, when He does speak to me and I know His reality and nearness, how unworthy I shall feel in His presence! How can I dare to reach out to Him as Magdalen did?

Oh, I dare only to ask this favor, dearest Mother, because I know from Your visitation at Fatima that You offer me Your Immaculate Heart with which to believe in Him, with which to trust Him, with which to love Him.

Dearest Mother of my Savior and my Mother, grant me, a poor sinner, this favor now. (Optional—decade prayer to the Father, p. 38).

†††

Second Glorious Mystery

The Mother He Left Behind

Our Lord knew the loneliness that would assail the apostles when He left them. He knew the desperation and fear that filled their hearts after the time of the crucifixion, and that would still tear at their weak natures until the great moment of Pentecost.

But that was not the only reason He left His Mother behind to be with them. Otherwise He would have left Her only until Pentecost. But He left Her for fifteen years!

She was to be the bridge. She was to be the Mother of the Church. She was to be the personal confidante of the first Pope. She was to be the consolation of the beloved disciple who had stood with Her at the foot of the cross, and the inspiration of the fiery apostle who had persecuted the new Church.

Certainly after Our Lord disappeared into heaven, having told them all that it was expedient that He go but that He would send the Paraclete who would make all things known to them, what a sense of comfort must have filled the hearts of the apostles when they realized that He had left His Mother with them! As the days went on, She was gathered with them in prayer at the cenacle, awaiting the fulfillment of Our Lord's great promise.

What a tremendous bond of love and trust must have developed in the hearts of those first members of the Church for their Mother! Today the world is forgetting this mystery of Mary's importance in the Church. Many cannot understand why it is that God sent the Mother of the Church at La Salette, at Lourdes, and finally at Fatima, with the apocalyptic messages of our times.

Pope Paul VI had to remind the world almost forcibly of Her importance at the end of the last session of the Ecumenical Council by officially proclaiming Her what She has always been, Mother of the Church, while simultaneously announcing that he was sending a special mission to Fatima to confer upon that site where She showed Herself Mother of the Church in our own time, the gift of the Golden Rose with the inscription: "We confide the entire Church to You."

This is what Our Lord did when He ascended into heaven, so is it any real surprise that the Holy Father repeated this now? Is it any wonder that we should turn to Mary, here in the presence of Jesus exposed, to find Her heart with which to worthily honor Him? Find a love to return His love? Find a trust worthy of His Infinite Goodness?

Certainly the closer we come to Mary, the closer we are certain to come to Christ. Even though He is human, He is also divine. I have no hope of grasping the greatness of this mystery unless I associate it with the mystery of a human being like myself who was exempted from original sin. I cannot hope to enter into this mystery unless I enter into the mystery of Her Immaculate Heart.

O, dearest Mother, my Mother and Mother of the Church, even as You were physically present with the first disciples in the cenacle after the resurrection, be present to me now as I find myself here in the physical presence of Your divine Son.

Obtain for me now, as I pray these next ten salutations, a sense of my responsibility in the Church, of my oneness with the other members gathered here before the Blessed Sacrament with me, and living in any circumstance, in any part of this city, this state, this nation, this world.

You appealed to me at Fatima, dearest Mother, to pray for the conversion of sinners, to accept my responsibility as a member of the Mystical Body of Christ. How can I fulfill this request unless You help me? (Optional—decade prayer to the Father, p. 38).

73.

Third Glorious Mystery

Fire

After their long days of waiting and of fearing, what sudden terror must have gripped the hearts of many of the disciples when the building trembled and the tremendous roar of thunder was heard!

But it was not the Roman Legions, or the armed mob of the Pharisees storming the building. It was a far different visitation! It was the fulfillment of the great promise of Christ when He said: "It is expedient that I go...I will send the Paraclete who will make all things known to you."

Fire appeared. The visible flame raged over Mary and then into tongues that leaped forth and appeared over the head of each person there!

With the fire came so many gifts that it astounded the world and resulted in a change in the whole course of humanity. Formerly weak, they were strong. Formerly dull in understanding, they were now brilliant. Formerly ignorant, they now spoke in many tongues. Formerly shaky in their love, they now loved enough to die for God and for the salvation of their fellow men.

Has Our Lady not promised us at Fatima a similar visitation? Today there are thousands huddled in concentration camps or in the secrecy of their homes behind the Iron and Bamboo Curtains, living in constant fear. But Our Lady has said that if enough persons will pray, the militant atheists will be converted.

How will this conversion take place except by a fiery storm of love from the Holy Spirit descending upon them?

Our Lady has promised that this evil that has been fomenting wars, and that could bring upon us the annihilation of entire nations, will be lifted if only enough persons will make sacrifices and will pray for the conversion of sinners. Is not the very event of Pentecost proof to us that Our Lady can and will keep Her promise?

Again at Fatima, She used fire to confirm the reality of Her promise. She promised that on a certain day, in a certain place, She would perform a public miracle so that "everyone may believe." On that day upwards of a hundred thousand people stared into the sky and saw a ball of fire which was so much like the sun that they described it as the sun.

They saw it dance in the sky and then suddenly plunge toward the earth, as though it were about to consume them and all the world around them. Each and every person in that vast throng was convinced that it was the end of the world. Just as suddenly as it seemed about to consume them, it gathered back into itself and staggered back into the sky.

Immediately everything around them which had been drenched by many hours of heavy rain, was dry. The sky had cleared and the sun was shining normally in the heavens.

Even as Our Lady could cause this tremendous fire to appear in the sky and fall upon the mountain at Fatima, certainly She can obtain from God such a tremendous fire of the Holy Spirit that could convert not only the Communists, but could change the hearts of the most wicked men. Above all, it could turn those who are weak in their faith, it could turn weaklings into giants, it could give us all the kind of love that we would be willing to die for God.

Is there anything we could more earnestly desire for these, our own days? Can't we identify ourselves at this moment with those who are imprisoned, with those who are praying behind locked doors, with those who read of God and think of God in secret?

Oh, how important is this night! Because so few have had the understanding.

I am not worthy to be here. I am no better than any of those who are not here. But I turn to You, dearest Mother, and remind You that it is because of Your appeal that I have come. I need You. Please lend me the fire of Your Immaculate Heart with which to call down the fire of the Holy Spirit—even as that fire called Him to be Your spouse and brought about the Incarnation—even as that fire called Him down to the cenacle to confirm all the disciples in the first Pentecost.

O, Mother of the Church, be my Mother now. As I recite these next ten salutations, with each one give me an increase of the gift of the Holy Spirit and make me a victim soul, an instrument to help bring about the great miracle which You promised at Fatima, the conversion of militant atheists and the peace of the world. (Optional—decade prayer to the Father, p. 38).

Fourth Glorious Mystery

Death

How many of the deaths tonight will be inglorious? In the early morning hours of this day, death wagons will roll through the streets of Calcutta and Benares in India to pick up the corpses of persons who died in the streets, unattended, unwept for.

Some will die tonight in concentration camps after years of torture and semi-starvation. They will have no priest. They will long have been without the Sacraments. They will long have endured the mockery of their faith. But even though they may be un-attended and dying in a most pitiable condition, if they have persevered, how glorious their deaths will be!

What will my own death be like? Will it come within a week, a month, a few years? Most certainly it will come. This is as certain as the fact that I am here.

In each of these Hail Marys I have been asking my Mother to pray for me at the hour of my death—but not just for me, but for all of us sinners. For while I need help at all times in my life, the hour of my death is my last chance for salvation. It is the last chance for everyone. Who can help those souls dying tonight in places such as Benares and Calcutta? Who can help those who die in concentration camps and prisons? Who can help those who die alone, without spiritual succor?

Only persons like myself—persons who are also part of the human family and who can reach through distances even to persons unknown with the tremendous power of human love, with the far greater power of prayer to the God who made us.

That is one of the most important reasons why I am here tonight. I am here because of the reality of death, which for many can be made glorious only if I and others like I remember to pray.

Was this not the most urgent, the most plaintive message of Our Lady at Fatima?

She showed the children a vision of hell, with souls falling into hell in such great numbers that it was like leaves falling from the trees in autumn, as she lamented: "So many souls are lost because there is no one to pray and to make sacrifices for them."

Now, as I come to the close of this night, in this mystery of Our Lady's own death, I plead with Her in a special way for the faith, the love, and the trust in God that will enable me to obtain the last-minute conversion of a thousand sinners.

What love surrounded Mary at the moment of Her death! What joys awaited Her as She was to be almost immediately raised back to life and taken bodily into heaven to reign with Her divine Son! She had endured the birth, the years of anxiety, the three days of loss, and finally the terrible fulfillment of Simeon's prophesy, when She witnessed Our Lord's passion, heard the pounding on the nails, and saw Him die.

She had endured the fifteen years of exile from Him after the ascension. She had humbly, in a thousand ways we can never know, aided the new Church, comforted the apostles in their distress, and anguished over the death of the first martyr. Now came that longed-for moment, the moment of Her own death.

Dearest Mother, I need not remind You tonight of all those who may not only die ingloriously, but may die in mortal sin—lost to the Passion of Your Son, lost to all the graces He brought to the world through You. It is You, dearest Mother, who at Fatima reminded me. You told me that we, the living, are our brothers' keepers. Only we, still exercising our free will, can raise the entire human family from its present distress. Only we can change that terrible statement you made at Fatima as you showed us hell: "There is no one to pray and to make sacrifice for them."

I am here this night, dearest Mother, to make that sacrifice, to say those prayers. But I am not worthy to be here. I am not worthy myself to have a glorious death. I tremble at the thought of my own final moments as I remember my weaknesses, my failures, and the possible fall that I may make tomorrow. It even has been known that some who make the all-night vigils and holy hours become the special object of Satan's hatred, and fall away not only from this holy practice, but into abominable habits of sin. Yes, dearest Mother, I am not worthy to be here, and I tremble for my own tomorrow.

However, I have heard your plea. I recall before my mind the vision of hell which the children of Fatima described. I can still hear echoing the words of little Jacinta; "O, if Our Lady had not been there I would have died of fright!" Forgetting my own misery, dearest Mother, I accede to Your request by giving this night in reparation for my sins and the sins of the world, I plead with You for a glorious death for a thousand souls now—that before this day is over, because of this vigil, a thousand souls who otherwise would be damned, will receive the grace of final contrition.

I ask this, dearest Mother, by virtue of Your own most glorious transition to Heaven. (Optional—decade prayer to the Father, p. 38).

Fifth Glorious Mystery

The World's Hope

In 1946 Pope Pius XII sent a personal Legate to Fatima (Cardinal Macella) and crowned the statue of Our Lady at the spot where She appeared, simultaneously proclaiming Her in a radio message to the world.

Then in 1954 the Holy Father caused the most venerable picture of Our Lady in Christendom to be carried from St. Mary Major's in Rome to St. Peter's, and there over the tomb of Peter he crowned that picture and instituted the Feast of the Queenship of Mary. In his decree the Holy Father said: "We are not instituting something new in the Church, but affirming something old...and I recall to you that I first crowned Her Queen of the World at Fatima."

So in a sense, we are living now in that moment of the flowering of Christianity which could be called the moment of Mary's Queenship. This is the moment of the world's hope. As Pope John XXIII put it: "Fatima is the hope of the world." Or to use another expression of "the Pope of Fatima," Pope Pius XII, which would seem incongruous against the backdrop of the atomic armament race: "We are in the springtime of history."

Yes, the great promise of Our Lady of Fatima far outweighs Her terrible prophesies of the second World War, and even of the annihilation of nations: "My Immaculate Heart will triumph, and an era of peace will be conceded to mankind."

But how will this reign of the Queenship of Mary be accomplished? Has the world even begun to recognize that it is by borrowing the fire of the Immaculate Heart of Mary that we can bring upon the earth the flaming love of His Sacred Heart? Or, to turn the analogy, is it not only by lighting our love with the fire of the Immaculate Heart that we can attract there the full flame of the love of Jesus?

The very title Queen implies power. We so often think of Our Lady as the humble virgin of Nazareth, the instrument of God's grace, the means by which He has come to the world. But we too rarely think of Her in the fulfillment of Her role as intermediary, in the fulfillment of Her position as the means of God's coming to the world.

We rarely think of Her in the fullness of Her power—a power so great that Christ acknowledged it by performing a miracle before His time at Her mere suggestion, and the first miracle in history at a predicted time and place in our very own day at

Fatima so that "everyone may believe." This is a dark hour for Satan, who trembles constantly in remembrance of the words God spoke in the Garden of Eden: "I shall place enmity between thee and the Woman, thy seed and Her seed, and thou shalt lie in wait for Her heel and She shall crush thy head."

How can we bring the power of our Queen into the world? We can do this by truly being Her "seed"— by responding to Her appeal at Fatima as obedient, loving children would do. She asked for our prayer and sacrifice, and this night have we given Her enough?

Oh no, dearest Mother, we want to give You all the nights, all the days, all the hours, all the minutes of our lives. We thank You for the grace of being here. We thank You for all the graces we have experienced in these passing moments. Now we long to become more efficient instruments of Your love, Your grace, Your intervention in the world. Since You are my Queen, take possession of all my faculties. Make my heart Your heart. Fill my imagination. Enlighten my understanding. Keep me ever conscious of the paradox of my complete unworthiness and yet of my tremendous power because I am Your child and You will hear my requests—and since You are a Queen with power over all things, when You hear me the world will change.

Final Prayer Before Closing Mass

Now I have ended my night with Your divine Son, fulfilling Your request for prayer and sacrifice. I have borrowed Your Immaculate Heart to love Him with Your love, to adore Him with Your faith, to pray to Him with Your trust and confidence.

But the greatest moment of all remains. Once again I am about to be present with You on Calvary, really and truly. Calvary is about to become present to me in the Sacrifice of the Mass.

When I attended the Sacrifice of the Mass at the opening of this vigil, I united my heart with Yours at the foot of the cross, You who are the Mother of suffering, the Co-redemptrix, the sorrowful one.

Now at this Sacrifice of the Mass, when it is the suffering Christ who is to become present on the altar when Calvary becomes present to me, I unite my poor heart with Your Immaculate Heart, not in its mystery of thorns but in its mystery of power.

To You, said St. Grignion de Montfort, have been confided the keys of the cellars of divine love. So when I kneel at the foot of the cross during this Sacrifice, I will be kneeling with the heart which the redeeming Christ cannot refuse. In that heart, dearest Mother, I place the salvation of a thousand souls who otherwise would be lost before this night is over were it not for this Sacrifice, for this prayer.

This is my gift to You, my Mother and Queen. This is my gift to my Redeemer: A thousand souls.

In these next ten salutations, I will ask You for two special favors:

First, dearest Mother, give me an understanding of my own unworthiness. I would not be here if I had not been called. I would not be here if, sometime in my life, I had not been given the star of Your devotion to guide me through the darkness, to lead me up out of the slough of evil into which I fell, and to bring me constantly back to the consuming love of Jesus and the greater faith in His true presence.

But Satan who so deplores my keeping Your request for the conversion of sinners, will not only do everything to prevent me from making a vigil, but will try to spoil it all by pointing out that there are not many people here, and that, therefore, I may be some special kind of person because I came. I can only overcome this kind of terrible temptation, dearest Mother, if Thou will obtain for me that sense of perspective and of right which filled Your heart when You explained before Elizabeth that Your soul magnified the Lord not because You were the Immaculate Conception, but because He who was mighty had recognized the nothingness, the lowliness of His handmaid.

Second, dearest Mother, having asked You to preserve me from every type of sin, especially the sin of pride, I ask You for a final time to lend me Your

Immaculate Heart, the heart of My Mother and Queen—
but as St. Therese said: "More a Mother than a Queen."

I want this Mass which I am about to attend to
be the most important of my entire life. No matter
how many times previously I have been privileged to
be present on Calvary in the Sacrifice of the Mass,
no matter how many times I may have this privilege
again in the days to come, I know that right now
I have only this one chance, this one moment right
now to speak to Our Lord as He hangs on the cross.
So give me all the virtues I need by filling my heart
with the virtues of Your Immaculate Heart, that Our
Lord may look down from the cross and behold not
unworthy me, but His own loving Mother, more a Mother
than a Queen—but with all the power of a queen
to vanquish sin, to drive Satan back into hell. (Optional—
decade prayer to the Father, p. 38).

Part 3.

ALTERNATIVE PROGRAMS AND PRAYERS

The fifteen decades of the Rosary require only three hours. Another two hours will be filled with the two Masses. This leaves *three or four additional hours to be planned.*

Those hours may include a penitential service, acts of consecration, reading of the promises of the Sacred Hearts, Chaplet of Mercy, etc.

Various books are available for appropriate readings and prayers. *Practices of Piety,* published by Two Hearts Media, is an excellent vigil booklet widely used in the Philippines. It is based on the nine offices of the Sacred Hearts.

One practice particularly appropriate at each vigil is to repeat, before the Blessed Sacrament, the first Friday-Saturday promises of their Sacred Hearts:

Promises of the Sacred Heart

Jesus Himself made the following 12 promises to St. Margaret Mary:

1. I will give them all the graces necessary in their state of life.

2. I will establish peace in their homes.

3. I will comfort them in all their afflictions.

4. I will be their secure refuge during life, and above all in death.

5. I will bestow abundant blessings upon all their undertakings.

6. Sinners will find in My Heart the source and the infinite ocean of mercy.

7. Tepid souls shall become fervent.

8. Fervent souls shall quickly mount to high perfection.

9. I will bless every place in which an image of My Heart shall be exposed and honored.

10. I will give to priests the gift of touching the most hardened hearts.

11. Those who shall promote this devotion shall have their names written in My Heart, never to be effaced.

12. I promise you in the excessive mercy of My Heart that My all-powerful love will grant to all those who communicate on the first Friday, in nine consecutive months, the grace of final penitence; they shall not die in My disgrace nor without receiving the Sacraments. My Divine Heart shall be their safe refuge in this last moment.

The Five First Saturdays

Our Lady said at Pontevedra: *"I promise to assist at the hour of death, with the graces needed, whoever on the First Saturday of five consecutive months shall:*

1. *Confess and receive Holy Communion;*

2. *recite five decades of the Rosary;*

3. *keep Me company for fifteen minutes while meditating on the mysteries of the Rosary;*

4. *have the intention of making reparation to Me."*

Meaning of the Promises

The first Friday promise of the Sacred Heart is that we will die in the State of Grace. The first Saturday promise of the Immaculate Heart is that we shall not only die in the State of Grace, but Our Lady will "assist" (be present) with all the graces and help necessary. (Many consider this to be a promise of a peaceful transition.)

Two years after Our Lady appeared at Fatima and said, *"I will come to ask for Communions of Reparation on the first Saturday,"* in a rescript in his own hand Pope Benedict XV granted *a plenary indulgence at the hour of death, under the condition of contritely invoking the name of Jesus, to "those who for once in their lifetime perform some special exercises of devotion in honor of the Blessed Virgin Immaculate, in order to make atonement for the blasphemies whereby the name and prerogatives of the Blessed Virgin are reviled, ON THE FIRST SATURDAYS of eight consecutive months."*

It was eighteen years *after* the Holy Father granted this indulgence that Our Lady came to ask for the *five* first Saturdays and to make Her great promise of Her assistance at the hour of death for those who complete this devotion.

OTHER PRAYERS

To the Holy Spirit:

Come, Holy Ghost, Creator blest,
And in our hearts take up Thy rest.
Come, with Thy grace and heavenly aid,
To fill the hearts which Thou hast made.
To fill the hearts which Thou hast made.

O Holy Spirit, the divine Spirit of light and love, I consecrate to Thee my understanding, heart, and will, my whole being for time and eternity. May my understanding be always submissive to Thy heavenly inspirations, and to the teaching of the Catholic

Church of which Thou are the infallible guide; and may my heart be ever inflamed with the love of God and of my neighbor; may my will be ever conformed to the divine will, and may my whole life be a faithful imitation of the life and virtues of Our Lord and Savior Jesus Christ to Whom the Father and Thee be honor and glory forever. Amen.

(Indulgence 600 days—Raccolta 289)

Prayers Taught at Fatima

O My Jesus, it is for love of You, in reparation for the offenses committed against the Immaculate Heart of Mary, and for the conversion of poor sinners!

My God, I believe, I adore, I trust and I love Thee! I beg pardon for those who do not believe, do not adore, do not trust, and do not love Thee.

Most Holy Trinity I adore Thee! My God, my God, I love Thee in the Most Blessed Sacrament.

O Most Holy Trinity, Father, Son, and Holy Ghost, I Adore Thee profoundly. I offer Thee the Most Precious Body, Blood, Soul, and Divinity of Jesus Christ, present In all the tabernacles of the world, In reparation for the outrages, sacrileges, and indifference by which He Is offended. By the Infinite Merits of the Sacred Heart of Jesus, and the Immaculate Heart of Mary, I beg the conversion of poor sinners.

My Jesus, forgive us our sins; save us from the fires of hell; lead all souls to heaven, especially those most in need of Thy mercy.

††††

Chaplet of Divine Mercy

Our Lord promised: **"Even if there were a sinner most hardened, if he were to recite this chaplet only once he would receive grace from My infinite mercy... I desire to grant unimaginable graces to those souls who trust in My mercy... Through the Chaplet you will obtain everything, if what you ask is compatible with My Will."**

The chaplet is recited on ordinary rosary beads beginning with the Our Father, one Hail Mary, and the Apostles' Creed. Then on the large bead before each decade:

Eternal Father, I offer You the Body, Blood, Soul, and Divinity of Your dearly beloved Son, Our Lord Jesus Christ, (response) *in atonement for our sins and those of the whole world.*

On the ten small beads of each decade:

For the sake of His sorrowful Passion, (response) *have mercy on us and on the whole world!*

In conclusion, say three times:

Holy God, Holy Mighty One, Holy Immortal One, have mercy on us and on the whole world.

O Blood and Water which gushed forth from the Heart of Jesus as a fountain of mercy for us, I trust in You!

Prayers From The Mass Of St. John:

Receive, O Holy Father, almighty and eternal God, this spotless Host, which I, Thy unworthy servant, offer unto Thee, my living and true God, for my own countless sins, offenses, and negligences, and for all here present, and also for all faithful Christians living and dead, that it may avail both for my own and their salvation unto life eternal. Amen.

We offer unto Thee, O Lord, the Chalice of salvation, beseeching Thy clemency, that it may ascend in the sight of Thy divine majesty with a sweet savor, for our own salvation and for that of the whole world. Amen.

The day before He suffered He took bread into His holy and venerable hands, and with eyes lifted up to heaven, unto Thee, God, His almighty Father, giving thanks to Thee, He blessed, broke, and gave it to His disciples, saying: Take and eat ye all of this,

FOR THIS IS MY BODY.

In like manner, after He had supped, taking also this excellent chalice into His holy and venerable hands, and giving thanks to Thee, He blessed and gave it to His disciples, saying: Take and drink ye all of this,

FOR THIS IS THE CHALICE OF MY BLOOD,
OF THE NEW AND ETERNAL TESTAMENT,
THY MYSTERY OF FAITH, WHICH SHALL BE
SHED FOR YOU AND FOR MANY
UNTO THE REMISSION OF SINS.

As often as ye do those things, ye shall do them in remembrance of Me.

STATIONS OF THE CROSS

Priest: In the name of the Father, and of the Son, and of the Holy Spirit.
All: Amen.

Priest: We adore You, O Christ, and we praise You.
All: Because by Your holy cross, You have redeemed the world.

Priest: With a humble spirit and a contrite heart, we offer this tribute of worship to You, Eternal Father, that it may bring You honor and glory, and profit us and all faithful Christians, both living and dead, in forgiving our sins, and attaining life everlasting.
All: Amen.

1st station:
JESUS IS CONDEMNED TO DEATH

Priest: He came unto His own.
All: And His own received Him not.

Priest: Pilate asked: What evil has He done? But they cried out: "Crucify Him."
All: "Crucify Him."

Priest: Savior of the world. Have mercy on us.
All: Have mercy on us.

Hymn: At the Cross Her station keeping
Stood the mournful Mother weeping,
Close to Jesus to the last.

89.

2nd station:
JESUS RECEIVES HIS CROSS

Priest: He humbled Himself being obedient unto death.
Even to death on the cross.
All: Even to death on the cross.

Priest: He bore the sins of many,
All: And prayed for all transgressors.

Priest: Savior of the world.
All: Have mercy on us.

Hymn: *Through Her heart, His sorrow sharing*
All His bitter anguish bearing,
Now at length the sword has passed.

3rd station:
JESUS FALLS. THE FIRST TIME

Priest: We thought of Him as a leper.
All: As one struck by God and afflicted.

Priest: God forbid that I should glory.
All: Save in the cross of Jesus Christ.

Priest: Savior of the world.
All: Have mercy of us.

Hymn: *Oh, how sad and sore distressed*
Was that Mother highly blest
Of the sole-begotten one!

4th station:
JESUS MEETS HIS BLESSED MOTHER

Priest: This Child is destined for the fall and rise of many,
All: And for a sign that shall be contradicted.

Priest: Your own soul,
All: A sword shall pierce.

Priest: Savior of the world.
All: Have mercy on us.

Hymn: Christ above in torment hangs;
She beneath, beholds the pangs
Of Her dying glorious Son.

5th station:
JESUS IS HELPED TO CARRY THE CROSS

Priest: They found a man of Cyrene named Simon.
All: Whom they forced to take up the cross.

Priest: Take up your cross daily.
All: And follow me.

Priest: Savior of the world.
All: Have mercy on us.

Hymn: Is there one who would not weep
Whelmed in miseries so deep,
Christ's dear Mother to behold?

6th station:
THE FACE OF JESUS IS WIPED BY VERONICA

Priest: By the sweat of your face, you shall eat bread.
All: Until your return to the dust of the earth.

Priest: May God have pity on us and bless us.
All: May He let His face shine upon us.

Priest: Savior of the world.
All: Have mercy on us.

Hymn: Can the human heart refrain
From partaking in Her pain,
In that Mother's pain untold.

7th station:
JESUS FALLS THE SECOND TIME

Priest: For our iniquities He was wounded.
All: For our sins He was bruised.

Priest: Unless the grain of wheat falls to the
ground and dies, it remains alone.
All: But if it dies, it brings forth much fruit.

Priest: Savior of the world.
All: Have mercy on us.

Hymn: Bruised, derided, cursed, defiled,
She beheld Her tender Child,
All with bloody scourges rent.

8th station:
JESUS SPEAKS TO THE WOMEN OF JERUSALEM

Priest: Daughters of Jerusalem, do not weep for Me
All: But for yourselves and your children.

Priest: Be imitators of Christ and walk in love.
All: As Christ loved us, and delivered Himself up
for us.

Priest: Savior of the world.
All: Have mercy on us.

Hymn: For the sins of His own nation
Saw Him hang in desolation,
Till His Spirit forth He sent.

9th station:
JESUS FALLS THE THIRD TIME

Priest: He has borne our infirmities.
All: And carried our sorrows.

Priest: He was ordered because it was His own.
All: And He opened not His mouth.

Priest: Savior of the world.
All: Have mercy on us.

Hymn: O Thou Mother, fount of love
Touch my spirit from above,
Make my heart with Thine accord.

10th station:

JESUS IS STRIPPED OF HIS GARMENTS

Priest: Upon Him was the chastisement that brought us peace.
All: By His bruises we are healed.

Priest: You know you were redeemed.
All: With the precious blood of Christ.

Priest: Savior of the world.
All: Have mercy on us.

Hymn: *Make me feel as Thou has felt*
Make my soul to glow and melt,
With the love of Christ the Lord.

11th station:

JESUS IS NAILED TO THE CROSS

Priest: At the third hour they crucified Him.
All: And Jesus said: "Father forgive them."

Priest: With Christ I am nailed to the cross.
All: I live no longer, but Christ lives in me.

Priest: Savior of the world.
All: Have mercy on us.

Hymn: *Holy Mother, pierce me through;*
In my heart each wound renew
Of my Savior crucified.

12th station:
JESUS DIES ON THE CROSS

Priest: If I be lifted up from the earth.
All: I will draw all things to Myself.

Priest: Christ died once for sins.
All: That He might bring us to God.

Priest: Savior of the world.
All: Have mercy of us.

Hymn: Let me share with Thee, His pain,
Who for all my sins was slain,
Who for me in torments died.

13th station:
JESUS IS TAKEN DOWN FROM THE CROSS

Priest: Purge out the old leaven.
All: For Christ, our Passover, has been sacrificed.

Priest: Consider yourselves as dead to sin.
All: But alive to God in Christ Jesus.

Priest: Savior of the world.
All: Have mercy on us.

Hymn: Let me mingle tears with Thee,
Mourning Him, who mourned for me,
All the days that I may live.

14th station:

JESUS IS LAID IN THE TOMB

Priest: We were buried with Him by baptism into death.
All: That we may walk in the newness of life.

Priest: If we have been united with Him in the likeness of His death.
All: So we shall be in the likeness of His resurrection.

Priest: Savior of the world.
All: Have mercy on us.

Hymn: Mine with Thee be that sad station
There to watch the great salvation,
Wrought upon the atoning tree.

CONCLUDING PRAYER AT THE ALTAR:

Priest: We adore You, O Christ, and we praise You.
All: Because by Your holy cross, You have redeemed the world.

Priest: Let us pray: O God, Who in order to drive the power of the enemy far from us, willed that Your Son should suffer for us on the cross, grant, we beseech You that we, who rejoice in honoring the same holy cross, may rejoice in Your loving care, and obtain the grace of resurrection. Through the same Christ, Our Lord.
All: Amen.

Priest: In the name of the Father, and of the Son, and of the Holy Spirit.

EXPOSITION: "O SAVING VICTIM" (O SALUTARIS)

O saving Victim, opening wide
The gate of heaven to man below!
Our foes press on from every side,
Thine aid supply, Thy strength bestow.

To Thy great name be endless praise,
Immortal Godhead, One in Three;
Oh, grant us endless length of days
In our true native land with Thee.

Amen.

LITURGICAL NIGHT PRAYERS

(Note: Known as "compline," these are the official
night prayers of the Church in the Divine Office.
Designate two sides of the congregation (to the left
and to the right) in reciting the psalms and let
each side alternate in reciting the verses.)

Priest: Lord, Your blessing, please. (Blessing)
May the all-powerful Lord grant us a peaceful
night and a perfect end.
All: Amen.

Priest: Brethren: Be sober, be watchful; for your
adversary the devil, as a roaring lion, goes
about seeking someone to devour. Resist
him, steadfast in the faith. Now on us, O
Lord, have mercy.
All: Thanks be to God.

Priest: Our help is in the name of the Lord.
All: Who made heaven and earth.

Priest: I confess to almighty God, to blessed Mary ever Virgin, to blessed Michael the Archangel, to blessed John the Baptist, to the holy Apostles Peter and Paul, to all the Saints and to you, brethren, that I have sinned through my fault, through my fault, through my most grievous fault. Therefore I beseech Blessed Mary ever Virgin, blessed Michael the Archangel, blessed John the Baptist, the holy Apostles Peter and Paul, all the Saints and you, brethren, to pray to the Lord our God for me.

All: Amen.

Priest: May almighty God have mercy on you, forgive you your sins, and bring you to life everlasting.

All: Amen.

Priest: May the almighty and merciful Lord grant us pardon, absolution, and remission of our sins.

All: Amen.

Priest: Make us turn to You, O God our Savior.

All: And cease being angry with us.

Priest: O God, come to my assistance.

All: O Lord, make haste to help me.

Priest: Glory be to the Father, and to the Son, and to the Holy Ghost.

All: As it was in the beginning, is now and ever shall be, world without end. Amen.

(Alleluia or...Praise to You, Lord.)

A

Antiphon: Aloud to the Lord I cried; and God will not forget to show mercy.

Psalm 76
UNCEASING PRAYER
(Let sides of congregation alternate)

Aloud to God I cry; aloud to God, to hear me;
on the day of my distress I seek the Lord.

By night my hands are stretched out without
flagging; my soul refuses comfort.

When I remember God, I moan; when I ponder,
my spirit grows faint.

You keep my eyes watchful; I am troubled and
cannot speak.

I consider the days of old; the years long past I
remember.

In the night I meditate in my heart; I ponder, and
my spirit broods:

"Will the Lord reject forever and nevermore be
favorable?

Will His kindness utterly cease, His promise fail
for all generations?

Has God forgotten pity? Does He in anger withhold
compassion?"

And I say, "This is my sorrow, that the right hand
of the Most High is changed."

I remember the deeds of the Lord; yes, I
remember Your wonders of old.

And I meditate on Your works; Your exploits I
ponder.

Glory be to the Father, Amen.

Psalm 76
GOD'S HOLINESS AND POWER

O God, your way is holy; what great god is there like our God?

You are the God who works wonders; among the peoples You have made known Your power.

With Your strong arm You redeemed Your people, the sons of Jacob and Joseph.

The waters saw You, O God; the waters saw You and shuddered; the very depths were troubled.

The clouds poured down water; the skies gave forth their voices; Your arrows also sped abroad.

Your thunder resounded in the whirlwind; Your lightning illumined the world; the earth quivered and quaked.

Through the sea was Your way, and Your path through the deep waters, though Your footsteps were not seen.

You led your people like a flock under the care of Moses and Aaron.

Glory be to the Father, and to the Son, and to the Holy Spirit. As it was in the beginning, is now, and ever shall be, world without end. Amen.

†††

Psalm 85
A PLEA IN GREATEST NEED

Incline Your ear, O Lord; answer me for I am afflicted and poor.

Keep my life, for I am devoted to You; save Your servant who trusts in You.

You are my God; have pity on me, O Lord, for to you I call all the day.

Gladden the soul of Your servant, for to You, O Lord, I lift up my soul.

For you, O Lord, are good and forgiving, abounding in kindness to all who call upon You.

Hearken, O Lord, to my prayer and attend to the sound of my pleading.

In the day of my distress I call upon You, for You will answer me.

There is none like you among the gods, O Lord, and there are no works like Yours.

All the nations You have made shall come and worship You, O Lord, and glorify Your name.

For You are great, and You do wondrous deeds; You alone are God.

Teach me, O Lord, Your way that I may walk in Your truth; direct my heart that it may fear Your name.

I will give thanks to You, O Lord my God, with all my heart, and I will glorify Your name forever.

Great has been Your kindness toward me; You have rescued me from the depths of the nether world.

O God, the haughty have risen up against me, and the company of fierce men seeks my life, nor do they set You before their eyes.

But You, O Lord, are a God merciful and gracious, slow to anger, abounding in kindness and fidelity.

Turn toward me, and have pity on me; give Your strength to Your servant, and save the son of Your handmaid.

Give me a proof of Your favor, that my enemies may see, to their confusion,

That You, O Lord, have helped and comforted me.

Glory be to the Father, and to the Son, and to the Holy Spirit,

As it was in the beginning, is now and ever shall be, world without end. Amen.

Antiphon: Aloud to the Lord I cried, and God will not forget to show mercy.

Hymn: Before the day is finished, Creator of the world, we earnestly ask of You that, in keeping with Your mercy, You be our protector and defense.

May no "ill dreams," no "nightly fears and fantasies" come near us. Hold in check our enemy that our bodies be not defiled.

Grant this, most loving Father and You, the only Son, equal to the Father and, with the Spirit, the Paraclete, reigning through the ages.

Amen.

JEREMIAH 14:9

Priest: You are in our midst, O Lord, Your name we bear; do not forsake us, O Lord our God.

All: Thanks be to God.

Priest: Into Your hands, O Lord, I commend my spirit. Into Your hands, O Lord, I commend my spirit.

All: You have redeemed us, O Lord, God of truth. I commend my spirit. Glory be to the Father, and to the Son, and to the Holy Spirit. As it was in the beginning, is now, and ever shall be, world without end. Into Your hands, O Lord, I commend my spirit.

Priest: Keep us, O Lord, as the pupil of Your eye.

All: Shelter us under the shadow of Your wings. Glory be to the Father and to the Son, and to the Holy Spirit. As it was in the beginning, is now, and ever shall be, world without end. Amen.

Antiphon: Protect us, Lord, while we are awake and safeguard us while we sleep, that we may keep watch with Christ and rest in peace. (P.T. Alleluia.)

LUKE 2:29-32

Now, Lord, You may dismiss Your servant in peace, according to Your word;

For my eyes have seen Your salvation, which You have set before all the nations.

As a light of revelation for the Gentiles and the glory of Your people Israel.

Glory be to the Father, and to the Son, and to the Holy Spirit.

As it was in the beginning is now, and ever shall he world without end. Amen.

Antiphon: Protect us, Lord, while we are awake and safeguard us while we sleep, that we may keep watch with Christ and rest in peace. (P.T. Alleluia.)

Priest: The Lord be with you.
All:　　And with your spirit.

Priest: O Lord, hear my prayer.
All:　　And let my cry come unto You.

LET US PRAY:
Visit this house, O Lord; keep the devil's wily influence away from it. Let Your holy Angels dwell here, to guard us in peace. And let Your blessing rest upon us always. This we ask of You through our Lord. Amen.

Priest: O Lord, hear my prayer.
All:　　And let my cry come unto You.

BLESSING:
Priest: May the all-powerful and merciful Lord, Father, Son, and Holy Spirit, bless and keep us.
All:　　Amen.

FROM FEBRUARY 2 THROUGH
WEDNESDAY OF HOLY WEEK

Antiphon: Hail, Queen of heaven; hail, Mistress of the Angels; hail, root of Jesse; hail, the gate through which the Light rose over the earth.

Rejoice, Virgin most renowned and of unsurpassed beauty. Farewell, Lady most comely. Prevail upon Christ to pity us.

Priest: Let me praise You, most holy Virgin.

All: Give me strength against Your enemies.

LET US PRAY:

O God of mercy, be the support of our weakness, and we shall celebrate in a fitting manner the memory of the holy Mother of God; thus by Her intercession may we rise from our sins! Through the same Christ, our Lord. Amen.

FROM EASTER SUNDAY THROUGH
FRIDAY WITHIN THE OCTAVE OF PENTECOST:

Antiphon: Queen of heaven, rejoice, alleluia. The Son Whom it was Your privilege to bear, alleluia, has risen as He said, alleluia. Pray to God for us, alleluia.

Priest: Rejoice and be glad, Virgin Mary, alleluia!

All: For the Lord has truly risen, alleluia!

LET US PRAY:

O God, You were pleased to give joy to the world through the Resurrection of Your Son, our Lord Jesus Christ. Grant, we beseech You, that through the mediation of the Virgin Mary, His Mother, we may come to possess the joys of life everlasting. Through the same Christ. Amen.

Priest: May the divine assistance remain always with us. And may the souls of the faithful departed,

All: Through the mercy of God, rest in peace. Amen.

LITANY OF THE SACRED HEART

Lord, have mercy on us.

(response) Christ, have mercy on us.

Lord, have mercy on us. Christ, hear us.

(response) Christ, graciously hear us.

God, the Father of Heaven, (HAVE MERCY ON US.)

God the Son, Redeemer of the world,   " " (repeat)

God the Holy Spirit,

Holy Trinity, one God,

Heart of Jesus, Son of the Eternal Father,

Heart of Jesus, formed by the Holy Ghost in the Womb of the Virgin Mother,

Heart of Jesus, substantially united to the Word of God,

Heart of Jesus, of Infinite Majesty,

Heart of Jesus, Sacred Temple of God,

Heart of Jesus, Tabernacle of the Most High,

Heart of Jesus, House of God and Gate of Heaven,

Heart of Jesus, burning furnace of charity,

Heart of Jesus, abode of justice and love,

Heart of Jesus, full of goodness and love,

Heart of Jesus, abyss of all virtues,

Heart of Jesus, most worthy of all praise,

Heart of Jesus, King and Center of all hearts,

Heart of Jesus, in whom are all the treasures of wisdom and knowledge,

Heart of Jesus, in whom dwells the fullness of Divinity,

Heart of Jesus, in whom the Father was well pleased,

Heart of Jesus, of whose fullness we have all received,

Heart of Jesus, desire of the everlasting hills,

Heart of Jesus, patient and most merciful,

Heart of Jesus, enriching all who invoke Thee,

Heart of Jesus, fountain of life and holiness,

Heart of Jesus, propitiation for our sins,

Heart of Jesus, loaded down with opprobrium,

Heart of Jesus, bruised for our offenses,

Heart of Jesus, obedient unto death,

Heart of Jesus, pierced with a lance,
Heart of Jesus, source of all consolation,
Heart of Jesus, our life and resurrection,
Heart of Jesus, our peace and reconciliation,
Heart of Jesus, victim of sin,
Heart of Jesus, salvation of those who trust in Thee,
Heart of Jesus, delight of all the saints,

Lamb of God, Who takest away the sins of the world,
Spare us, O Lord.
Lamb of God, Who takest away the sins of the world,
Graciously hear us, O Lord.
Lamb of God, Who takest away the sins of the world,
Have mercy on us.

Priest: Jesus, meek and humble of heart.
All: Make our hearts like unto Thine.

LET US PRAY:
O Almighty and Eternal God, look upon the Heart of
Your dearly beloved Son, and upon the praise and
satisfaction He offers You in behalf of sinners, and
being appeased, grant pardon to those who seek Your
mercy, in the name of the same Jesus Christ, Your
Son, Who lives and reigns with You, in the unity of
the Holy Spirit, world without end. Amen.

CONSECRATION OF THE HUMAN RACE
TO THE SACRED HEART OF JESUS

Most sweet Jesus, Redeemer of the human race, look
down upon us humbly prostrate before Thy altar. We
are Thine, and Thine we wish to be; but, to be more
surely united with Thee, behold each one of us freely
consecrates himself today to Thy Most Sacred Heart.

Many indeed have never known Thee; many too,
despising Thy precepts, have rejected Thee. Have mercy
on them all, most merciful Jesus, and draw them to
Thy Sacred Heart.

Be thou King O Lord, not only of the faithful who
have never forsaken Thee, but also of the prodigal

children who have abandoned Thee; grant that they may quickly return to their Father's house lest they die of wretchedness and hunger.

Be Thou King of those who are deceived by erroneous opinions, or whom discord keeps aloof, and call them back to the harbor of truth and unity of faith, so that soon there may be but one flock and one Shepherd.

Be Thou King of all those who are still involved in the darkness of idolatry or of Islamism, and refuse not to draw them all into the light and kingdom of God. Turn Thine eyes of mercy toward the children of that race, once Thy chosen people. Of old they called down upon themselves the Blood of the Savior; may it now descend upon them a laver of redemption and of life.

Grant, O Lord, to Thy Church assurance of freedom and immunity from harm; give peace and order to all nations, and make the earth resound from pole to pole with one cry: Praise to the Divine Heart that wrought our salvation; to It be glory and honor forever. Amen.

MEDITATION BEFORE THE BLESSED SACRAMENT

To please Me, My dear child, it is not necessary to know much; all that is required is to love Me much, to be deeply sorry for ever having offended Me and desirous of being ever faithful to Me in the future.

Speak to Me now as you would to your dearest friend. Tell me all that now fills your mind and heart. Are there any you wish to commend to Me?... Tell Me their names, and tell Me what you would wish Me to do for them. Do not fear, ask for much; I love generous hearts, which, forgetting themselves, wish well to others.

Ask Me many graces for yourself. Are there not many you would wish to name, that would make you happier, more useful and pleasing to others, and more worthy of My love?...Tell Me them with humility, knowing how poor you are without them, how unable to gain them by yourself; ask for them with much love, that they may make you more pleasing to Me.

With all a child's simplicity, tell Me how self-seeking you are, how proud, vain, irritable, how cowardly in sacrifice, how lazy in work, uncertain in your good resolutions...and then ask Me to bless and crown your efforts. Poor child, fear not, blush not at the sight of so many failings; there are Saints in Heaven who had the faults you have; they came to Me lovingly, they prayed earnestly to me— and My grace has made them good and holy in My sight.

You should be Mine, body and soul—fear not, therefore, to ask of Me gifts of body and mind, health, judgment, memory and success—ask for them for My sake—that God may be glorified in all things. I can grant everything...and never refuse to give what may make a soul dearer to Me and better able to fulfill the will of God.

Have you no plans for the future which occupy perhaps distress, your mind?...Tell Me your hopes— your fears. It is about your future state?...your position among My creatures?...some good you wish to bring to others? In what shall I help and bless your good will?

And what crosses have you—my dear child? Have they been many and heavy ones? Has someone caused you pain?...someone wounded your selflove?... slighted you?...injured you? Lay your head upon My breast, and tell Me how you suffered. Have you felt that some have been ungrateful to you—and unfeeling toward you? Tell Me all, and in the warmth of My Healt you will find strength to forgive and even to forget that they have ever wished to pain you.

And—what fears have you, My child?... My providence shall comfort you; never abandon you. Are some growing cold in the interest and love they had for you?... Pray to me for them; I will restore them to you, if it be better for you and your sanctification.

Have you not some happiness to make known to Me?... What has happened, since you came to Me last, to console you, to gladden and give you joy. What was it?...a mark of true friendship you received?... a success, unexpected and almost unhoped for?...a fear suddenly taken away from you?...and did you not remember the while, that in all, it was My will, My love—that brought all that your heart has been so glad to have? It was My hand, My dear child, that guided and prepared all for you. Look to Me now, My child, and say, "Dear Lord, I thank you."

You will soon leave Me now—what promises can you make Me?... Let them be sincere ones, humble ones, full of love and desire to please Me. Tell Me how carefully you will avoid every occasion of sin.

Promise Me to be kind to the poor, loving for My sake, to friends, forgiving to your enemies, and charitable to all...not in word alone and actions... but in your very thought. When you have little love for your neighbor, whom you see, you are forgetting Me, who am hidden from you.

Love all My saints; seek the help of your Holy Guardian Angel. Love, above all, My own dear glorious Mother. She is your mother. O love Her, speak to Her often and She will bring you to Me, and for Her sake I will love and bless you more each day.

Return soon to Me again...but come with your heart empty of the world, for I have many more favors to give, more than you can know of...bring your heart so that I may fill it with many gifts of My love. My peace be with you.

PRAYERS FROM SCRIPTURE

Hymn..."PRAISE TO THE LORD"

Praise to the Lord, The Almighty, the King of Creation;
O my soul, Praise Him, for He is our Health and Salvation.
All you who hear, now to the altar draw near;
Join in profound adoration.
Praise to the Lord, let us offer our gifts at the altar.
Let not our sins and offenses, now cause us to falter.
Christ, the High Priest, bids us all join in His feast,
Victims with Him on the altar.

Praise to the Lord, O let all that is in us adore Him.
All that has life and breath, come now rejoicing before Him.
Let the "Amen" sound from His people again,
As we here worship before Him.

First Reading...ISAIAH 2:2-5

RECITATION OF PSALM 61

Priest: Only in God does my soul rest—from Him comes my salvation.
All: He only is my rock and my salvation, my stronghold; I shall not be disturbed at all.

Priest: How long will you set upon a man and all together beat him down as though he were a sagging fence, a battered wall.
All: Truly, from my place on high they plan to dislodge me; they delight in lies; they bless with their mouths, but inwardly they curse.

Priest: Only in God be at rest, my soul, for from Him comes my hope.

All: He only is my rock and my salvation, my stronghold; I shall not be disturbed.

Priest: With God is my safety and my glory.

All: He is the rock of my strength; my refuge is in God.

Priest: Trust in Him at all times, O my people! Pour out your hearts before Him.

All: God is our refuge!

Priest: Only a breath are mortal men; an illusion are men of rank.

All: In a balance they prove lighter, all together, than a breath.

Priest: Trust not in extortion; in plunder, take no empty pride.

All: Though wealth abounds, set not your heart upon it.

Priest: One thing God said; these two things which I heard: that power belongs to God,

All: And Yours, O Lord, is kindness; and that You render to everyone according to his deeds.

Priest: Glory be to the Father, and to the Son, and to the Holy Spirit.

All: As it was in the beginning, is now, and ever shall be, world without end. Amen.

Hymn..."O GOD, ALMIGHTY FATHER"

O God, Almighty Father, Creator of all things, The Heavens stand in wonder, while earth, Thy glory sings.

CHORUS: O most Holy Trinity, undivided unity; Holy God, Mighty God—God immortal, be adored.

O Jesus, Word Incarnate, Redeemer most adored, All glory, praise, and honor be Thine, Our Sovereign Lord.

CHORUS: O most Holy Trinity....

O God, the Holy Spirit, Who lives within our soul, Send forth Thy light and lead us, to our eternal goal.

CHORUS: O most Holy Trinity....

Second reading...MATTHEW 5:1-12

RECITATION OF PSALM 111

Priest: Happy the man who fears the Lord, who greatly delights in His commands.
All: His posterity shall be mighty upon the earth; the upright generation shall be blessed.

Priest: Wealth and riches shall be in his house; his generosity shall endure forever.
All: He dawns through the darkness, a light for the upright; he is gracious and merciful and just.

Priest: Well for the man who is gracious and lends, who conducts his affairs with justice.
All: He shall never be moved; the just man shall be in everlasting remembrance.

Priest: An evil report he shall not fear; his heart is firm, trusting in the Lord.

All: His heart is steadfast; he shall not fear till he looks down upon his foes.

Priest: Lavishly, he gives to the poor; his generosity shall endure forever; his horn shall be exalted in glory.

All: The wicked man shall see it and be vexed; he shall gnash his teeth and pine away; the desire of the wicked shall perish.

Priest: Glory be to the Father, and to the Son, and to the Holy Spirit.

All: As it was in the beginning, is now, and ever shall be, world without end. Amen.

Hymn...'HOLY, HOLY, HOLY, LORD GOD ALMIGHTY"

Holy, holy, holy! Lord God Almighty!
Early in the morning, our song shall rise to Thee.
Holy, holy, holy! Merciful and mighty,
God in three persons, blessed Trinity.

Holy, holy, holy! Though the darkness hide Thee,
Though the eye of sinful man, Thy glory may not see.
Only Thou art holy; there is none beside Thee,
Perfect in power, in love, and purity.

Holy, holy, holy! Lord God Almighty!
All Thy works shall praise Thy name, in earth and sky, and sea.
Holy, holy, holy! Merciful and mighty,
God in three persons, blessed Trinity.

Priest: HOMILY

RECITATION OF PSALM 121

Priest: I rejoiced because they said to me, "We will go up to the house of the Lord."
All: And now we have set foot within your gates, O Jerusalem—Jerusalem, built as a city with compact unity.

Priest: To it the tribes go up, the tribes of the Lord, according to the decree for Israel, to give thanks to the name of the Lord.
All: In it are set up judgment seats, seats for the house of David.

Priest: Pray for the peace of Jerusalem! May those who love you prosper.
All: May peace be within your walls, prosperity in your buildings.

Priest: Because of my relatives and friends I will say, "Peace be within you!"
All: Because of the house of the Lord, our God, I will pray for your good.

Priest: Glory be to the Father, and to the Son, and to the Holy Spirit.
All: As it was in the beginning, is now, and ever shall be, world without end. Amen.

Let Us Pray...

Priest: Save Thy servants.
All: We hope in Thee, O our God.

Priest: Let not the enemy prevail against us.
All: Nor the son of iniquity have power to hurt us.

Priest: O Lord, deal not with us according to our sins.
All: Nor punish us according to our inquities.

Priest: Let us pray for the sovereign Pontiff.
All: The Lord preserve him and give him life; and make him blessed upon the earth; and deliver him from the will of his enemies.

Priest: Let us pray for our benefactors.
All: Grant, O Lord, for Thy Name's sake, to reward with eternal life, all those who do us good. Amen.

Priest: Let us pray for the faithful departed.
All: Eternal rest grant unto them, O Lord, and let perpetual light shine upon them.

Priest: May they rest in peace.
All: Amen.

Priest: For our absent brethren.
All: Save Thy servants who hope in Thee, O my God.

Priest: Send them help, O Lord, from Thy holy place.
All: And from Sion protect him.

Priest: O Lord, hear my prayer.
All: And let my cry come unto Thee.

Priest: The Lord be with you.
All: And with your spirit.

Priest: **Let us pray...**

Hymn..."GOD IS LOVE"

All:　God is love and he who abides in love abides in God—and God in him.

Chanter: The love of Christ has gathered us together—let us rejoice and be glad.
All:　(repeat) "God is love..."

Chanter: By this shall they know that we are His disciples—if we have love one for another.
All:　(repeat) "God is love..."

Chanter: Owe no man anything except to love one another—for he who loves his neighbor will fulfill the whole law.
All:　(repeat) "God is love..."

Chanter: O carry one another's burden—and so you will fulfill the Law of Christ.
All:　(repeat) "God is love..."

Chanter: The cup of blessing which we bless—is it not the sharing of the Blood of Christ?
All:　(repeat) "God is love..."

BLESSED SACRAMENT PROCESSION

Hymn..."JESUS, MY LORD"

Jesus, my Lord, my God, my All!
How can I love Thee as I ought?
And how revere this wondrous gift,
So far surpassing hope or thought?

Refrain: Sweet Sacrament, we Thee adore! Oh, make us love Thee, more and more—Oh, make us love Thee, more and more.

Had I but Mary's sinless heart
To love Thee with, my dearest King!
Oh, with what bursts of fervent praise
Thy goodness, Jesus, would I sing!

Refrain: "Sweet Sacrament, we Thee..."

Thy Body, Soul, and Godhead, all!
O mystery of love divine!
I cannot compass all I have,
For all Thou hast and art, are mine.

Refrain: "Sweet Sacrament, we Thee..."

Sound, sound His praises higher still,
And come, ye angels, to our aid;
'Tis God! 'Tis God! the very God,
Whose power, both man and angels, made!

Refrain: "Sweet Sacrament, we Thee..."

Hymn..."SING, MY TONGUE" (PANGE LINGUA GLORIOSI)

Sing, my tongue! Acclaim Christ present.
Veiled within this sacred Sign,
Precious blood and risen body,
Under forms of bread and wine.
Blood once shed for man's redemption,
By his king, of David's line.

Heaven's promised Gift to mankind,
Born to Virgin full of grace,
Plants the seed of faith securely,
While he dwells with Adam's race.
Ends His mission, leaves a symbol,
Of the death He will embrace.

Dining with His twelve apostles
On the night before He died,
Taking for the Paschal supper
Foods the Law had specified.
Lo, He sets new bread before them,
Handing each, Christ crucified.

Word made flesh makes bread His body,
Consecrates it, by His word.
Wine becomes the blood of Jesus,
He it is whose voice is heard.
Minds in doubt need faith's assurance;
God who spoke can not have erred.

Bowing low, then, offer homage
To a Sacrament so great!
Here is new and perfect worship;
All the old must terminate.
Senses cannot grasp this marvel;
Faith must serve to compensate.

Praise and glorify the Father,
Bless His Son's lifegiving name,
Singing Their eternal Godhead,
Power, majesty and fame,
Offering Their Holy Spirit
Equal worship and acclaim. Amen.

Rosary Hymns

For the joyful and glorious mysteries, the "AVE" of
Fatima or Lourdes is recommended to be sung at
the end of each decade. For the sorrowful mysteries,
sing one verse of the hymn below, after each decade:

1. At the Cross Her station keeping,
   Stood the mournful Mother weeping,
   Close to Jesus to the last.

2. Through Her heart, His sorrow sharing,
   All His bitter anguish bearing,
   Now at length the sword has passed.

3. Oh, how sad and sore distressed,
   Was that Mother highly blest,
   Of the sole-begotten one!

4. Christ above in torment hangs,
   She beneath beholds the pangs,
   Of Her dying glorious Son.

5. Is there one who would not weep,
   Whelmed in miseries so deep,
   Christ's dear Mother to behold?

PROCESSION WITH OUR LADY'S STATUE

Hymn..."HAIL HOLY QUEEN"

Hail, holy Queen enthroned above, O Maria!
Hail Mother of mercy, and of love, O Maria!
Chorus::   Triumph, all ye cherubim,
                Sing with us, ye seraphim!
                Heaven and earth resound the hymn.
                Salve, salve, salve Regina!

Our life, our sweetness here below, O Maria!
From You all grace and comfort flow, O Maria!
Chorus::   Triumph, all...

Our Advocate with God on high, O Maria!
To You our pleading voices cry, O Maria!
Chorus::   Triumph, all...

Hymn..."IMMACULATE MARY"

Immaculate Mary, Your praises we sing,
You reign now with Christ, our Redeemer and King.
Ave, Ave, Ave—Maria. Ave, Ave, Ave—Maria.

In heaven the blessed Your glory proclaim.
On earth we, Your children, invoke Your sweet name.
Ave...

We pray You, O Mother, may God's will be done.
We pray for His glory, may His kingdom come.
Ave...

We pray for our Mother, the Church upon earth,
And bless, holy Mary, the land of our birth.
Ave...

Hymn..."DAILY, DAILY SING TO MARY"

Daily, Daily, sing to Mary,
Sing my soul, Her praises due.
All Her feasts, Her actions honor,
With the heart's devotion true.

Lost in wond'ring contemplation
Be Her majesty confessed.
Call Her Mother, call Her virgin,
Happy Mother, virgin blessed.

She is mighty to deliver,
Call Her, trust Her, lovingly.
When the tempest rages round you,
She will calm the troubled sea.

Gifts of heaven, She has given,
Noble lady, to our race.
She, the Queen, who decks Her subjects,
With the light of God's own grace.

MATINS—LITURGICAL, MORNING PRAYERS

—LITTLE OFFICE OF THE BLESSED VIRGIN MARY—

Priest: Hail, Mary, full of grace, the Lord is with Thee.
Blessed art Thou among women and blessed is the
fruit of Thy womb, Jesus.
All: Holy Mary, Mother of God, pray for us
sinners, now and at the hour of our death. Amen.

Priest: You shall open my lips, O Lord.
All: And my mouth shall show forth Your praise.

Priest: Incline unto my aid, O God.
All: O Lord, make haste to help me.

Priest: Glory be to the Father, and to the Son, and to the Holy Spirit,
All: As it was in the beginning, is now, and ever shall be, world without end. Amen.

ALLELUIA
(During Lent...Praise be to Thee,
O Lord, King of endless glory.)

Priest: Hail, Mary, full of grace, the Lord is with You.
All: Hail, Mary, full of grace, the Lord is with You.

Priest: Come, let us rejoice...let us rejoice unto Him.
All: Hail, Mary, full of grace, the Lord is with You.

Priest: For the Lord is a great God...and the heights of the mountains are His.
All: The Lord is with You.

Priest: The sea is His...and the sheep of His hand.
All: Hail, Mary full of grace, the Lord is with You.

Priest: Do not harden your hearts as they were hardened once at Meribah.
All: The Lord is with You.

Priest: Forty years long I was offended, they shall not enter into my rest.
All: Hail, Mary, full of grace, the Lord is with You.

Priest: Glory be to the Father, and to the Son, and to the Holy Spirit. As it was in the beginning, is now, and ever shall be, world without end. Amen.
All: The Lord is with You.

> The Lord, whom earth, and sea, and sky,
> With one adoring voice proclaim;
> Who rules them all in majesty;
> Enclosed Himself in Mary's frame.

Lo, in a humble virgin's womb,
Overshadowed by Almighty power;
He whom the stars, and sun, and moon,
Each serve in their appointed hour.

Oh Mother blest, to whom was given
Within Thy body to contain,
The Architect of earth and heaven,
Whose hands the universe sustain.

To Thee was sent an angel down,
In Thee the Spirit was enshrined;
Of Thee was born that mighty one,
The long-desired of all mankind.

Oh Jesus, born of virgin bright,
Immortal glory be to You;
Praise to the Father infinite,
And Holy Spirit eternally. Amen.

The following psalms are to be said on Saturday:
   Antiphon: Rejoice, O Virgin Mary

Psalm 95—(Alternate Phrases)

Sing to the Lord a new song, sing to the Lord,
all you lands of the earth.
Sing to the Lord, bless His name, proclaim His
salvation from day to day.

Tell His glory among the heathen, His wonders
among all peoples.
For the Lord is great and all worthy of praise;
He is to be feared above all gods.

For all the gods of the gentiles are idols, but the
Lord made the heavens.
Majesty and beauty go before Him; might and
glory are in His holy dwelling-place.

Give to the Lord, you kindreds of the peoples, give to the Lord glory and might; give to the Lord the glory of His name.

Offer sacrifice and go into His courts; adore the Lord in holy attire.

Tremble before Him, all the earth; say among the heathen: The Lord reigns.

He has established the world, so that it be not moved: He rules the people with justice.

Let the heavens be glad, and let the earth rejoice; let the sea roar and the fullness thereof; let the field exult and all that is therein.

Then all the trees of the forest shall be joyful before the Lord, for He comes...for He comes to rule the earth.

He will rule the world with justice, and the peoples with His truth.

Glory be to the Father, and to the Son, and to the Holy Spirit,

As it was in the beginning, is now, and ever shall be, world without end. Amen.

ttt

Antiphon: Rejoice, O Virgin Mary. You alone have destroyed all heresies in the whole world.

Antiphon: Vouchsafe, that I may praise You, O Sacred Virgin. Give me strength against Your enemies.

Psalm 96

The Lord reigns: let the earth rejoice, let many islands be glad.

Clouds and darkness surround Him, justice and right are the foundation of His throne.

Fire goes before Him, and burns up His enemies round about.

His lightnings illumine the world; the earth sees and trembles.

The mountains melt like wax before the Lord, before the ruler of the whole earth.

The heavens proclaim His justice, and all peoples see His glory.

All are confounded that worship graven images and that glory in idols; all the gods fall down before Him.

Sion hears and is glad, and the cities of Juda rejoice because of Your judgments, O Lord.

For You, O Lord, are most high over all the earth, supremely eminent among all the gods.

The Lord loves them that hate evil; He watches over the souls of His saints, He rescues them from the hand of the wicked.

Light springs forth for the just man, and gladness for the upright of heart.

Rejoice, you just, in the Lord, and glorify His holy name.

Glory be to the Father, and to the Son, and to the Holy Spirit,

As it was in the beginning, is now, and ever shall be, world without end. Amen.

✝✝✝

Antiphon: Vouchsafe that I may praise You, O Sacred Virgin. Give me strength against Your enemies.

Antiphon: After childbirth, You did remain a pure virgin. Intercede for us, O Mother of God.

125.

(During Advent—*Antiphon:* The angel of the Lord.)

Psalm 97

Sing to the Lord a new song, because He has done wondrous things.
His right hand, and His holy arm, have prepared for Him the victory.

The Lord has made known His salvation; He has revealed His justice in the sight of the heathen.
He has remembered His goodness and faithfulness toward the house of Israel.

All the ends of the earth have seen the salvation of Our God.
Shout joyfully to the Lord, all you lands, be glad and rejoice and make melody.

Make melody to the Lord with the harp, with the harp and the sound of the psaltery,
Let the sea roar and the fullness thereof, the world and those that dwell therein.

Let the rivers clap their hands, let the mountains rejoice together.
Before the Lord...because He comes, because He comes to rule the earth.

He will rule the world with justice and the peoples with fairness.
Glory be to the Father, and to the Son, and to the Holy Spirit:

As it was in the beginning, is now, and ever shall be, world without end. Amen.

Antiphon: After childbirth, You did remain a pure virgin. Intercede for us, O Mother of God.

(In Advent *Antiphon:* The angel of the Lord announced unto Mary, and She conceived of the Holy Spirit.)

Priest: Grace is shed forth on Your lips.
All: Therefore has God blessed You forever.

OUR FATHER, etc. (Silently)

Priest: And lead us not into temptation.
All: But deliver us from evil.

Priest: By the prayers and merits of the Blessed Mary ever Virgin, and of all the Saints, may the Lord bring us to the kingdom of heaven.
All: Amen.

Priest: Pray, a blessing. May the Virgin Mary, with Her loving Child, bless us.
All: Amen.

LECTOR—LESSON 1.
Little Office of Blessed Virgin Mary

Priest: In all these I sought rest, have mercy on us.
All: Thanks be to God.

Priest: O holy and immaculate virginity, with what praises I shall extol Thee, I know not.
All: For He whom the heavens could not contain, rested in Your bosom.

Priest: Blessed are You among women, and blessed is the fruit of Your womb.
All: For He whom the heavens could not contain, rested in Your bosom.

Priest: Pray, a blessing. May the Virgin of virgins Herself intercede for us with the Lord.
All: Amen.

127.

LESSON II

Priest: And so I was established. ...But You, Lord,
have mercy on us.
All: Thanks be to God.

Priest: Blessed are You, O Virgin Mary, who did
bear the Lord, the Creator of the world:
All: You were the Mother of Him who made You,
and You remained a virgin forever.

Priest: Glory be to the Father, and to the Son, and
to the Holy Spirit.
All: You were the Mother of Him who made You,
and You remain a virgin forever.

Priest: Pray, a blessing. Through the virgin Mother,
may the Lord grant unto us salvation and peace.
All: Amen.

LESSON III

Priest: I was exalted like a cedar. ...But You, Lord,
have mercy on us.
All: Thanks be to God.
(Next to be omitted when TE DEUM is said)
Surely You are happy, O holy Virgin Mary, and
most worthy of all praise; for out of You arose
the Son of Justice, Christ our God.

Priest: Pray for the people, mediate for the clergy,
intercede for the consecrated women. Let all
experience Your assistance, whoever celebrates Your
holy commemoration.
All: For out of You arose the Son of Justice,
Christ our God.

Priest: Glory be to the Father, and to the Son,
and to the Holy Spirit.
All: Christ our God.

TE DEUM

We praise You, O God; we acknowledge You to be the Lord.

All the earth does worship You, the Father everlasting.

To You all angels cry aloud, the heavens and all the powers therein.

To You cherubim and seraphim, continually do cry:

Holy, holy, holy, Lord God of Sabaoth. Heaven and earth are full of the majesty of Your glory.

The glorious choir of the Apostles praise You.

The admirable company of the Prophets praise You.

The Holy Church throughout all the world does acknowledge You.

The Father of an infinite majesty, Thy adorable, true and only Son.

Also the Holy Spirit, the Comforter.

You are the King of Glory, O Christ.

You are the everlasting Son of the Father.

When You took upon You to deliver man, You did not abhor the Virgin's womb.

When You had overcome the sting of death, You did open the kingdom of heaven to all believers.

You sit at the right hand of God, in the glory of the Father.

We believe that You will come to be our Judge.

We pray You, therefore, help Your servants, whom You have redeemed with Your precious blood.

Make them to be numbered with Your Saints in glory everlasting.

O Lord, save Your people and bless Your inheritance. Govern them and lift them up forever.

Day by day we magnify You. And we praise Your name forever; yes, forever and ever.

Vouchsafe, O Lord, this day to keep us without sin. O Lord, have mercy upon us, have mercy upon us.

O Lord, let Your mercy be upon us, as we have hoped in You. O Lord, in You have I hoped, let me not be confounded forever.

— AMEN —

SCRIPTURE SERVICE IN HONOR OF SACRED HEART

Reading from John 14-17
(All kneel for silent prayer)

Priest: Let us stand and respond to the word of God. Bless the Lord, O my soul, and all that is within me, bless His holy name.
All: Put me as a seal upon Thy heart, as a seal upon Thy arm, for love is strong as death.

Priest: Bless the Lord, O my soul, and forget not all His benefits, who forgives all thy faults, who heals all thy diseases.
All: Put me as a seal upon Thy heart, as a seal upon Thy arm, for love is strong as death.

Priest: Who redeems thy life from destruction, who covers thee with favor and kindness.
All: Put me as a seal upon Thy heart, as a seal upon Thy arm, for love is strong as death.

Priest: Who fills thy life with good things; thy youth is renewed like the eagles.

All: Put me as a seal upon Thy heart, as a seal upon Thy arm, for love is strong as death.

Priest: The Lord is merciful and gracious, slow to anger, and plenteous in mercy.

All: Put me as a seal upon Thy heart, as a seal upon Thy arm, for love is strong as death.

Priest: He contends not with us according to our sins, nor does He repay us according to our faults.

All: Put me as a seal upon Thy heart, as a seal upon Thy arm, for love is strong as death.

Priest: For as much as heaven is high above the earth, so His mercy prevails towards them who fear Him.

All: Put me as a seal upon Thy heart, as a seal upon Thy arm, for love is strong as death.

Priest: As far as the east is from the west, so far does He remove our offenses from us.

All: Put me as a seal upon Thy heart, as a seal upon Thy arm, for love is strong as death.

Priest: Just as the father has compassion on his children, so has the Lord compassion on those who fear Him.

All: Put me as a seal upon Thy heart, as a seal upon Thy arm, for love is strong as death.

STAND FOR THE GOSPEL OF ST. JOHN
(Reading from the Bible)

PRIEST'S HOMILY

Priest: Let us stand and respond to the Word of God. Heart of Jesus, obedient unto death.

All: Have mercy on us.

Priest: (followed by all responding)
Heart of Jesus, pierced with a lance, (response)
Heart of Jesus, source of all consolation,
Heart of Jesus, our life and resurrection,
Heart of Jesus, our peace and reconciliation,
Heart of Jesus, victim of sin,
Heart of Jesus, salvation of those who trust in Thee,
Heart of Jesus, hope of those who die in Thee,
Heart of Jesus, delight of all the Saints,

All: O God, who in the Heart of Thy son, wounded by our sins, mercifully bestows upon us the infinite wealth of Thy love, grant, we beseech Thee, that by honoring it with fitting devotion, we may fulfill our duty of worthy reparation, through the same God, Jesus Christ, Thy Son, who lives and reigns with Thee in the unity of the Holy Spirit, God, world without end. Amen.

LAUDS FROM OFFICE OF THE BLESSED SACRAMENT

(All stand and recite the
Our Father and the Hail Mary silently.)
Make the Sign of the Cross when the Priest says:

Priest: Make haste, O God, to deliver me.
All: Make haste to help me, O Lord.

Priest: Glory be to the Father, and to the Son, and to the Holy Spirit,
All: As it was in the beginning, is now, and ever shall be, world without end. Amen. Alleluia.

Antiphon: Wisdom has built her a house, she has mingled her wine, she has also furnished her table.
(At Easter time, add—Alleluia.)

The Lord has reigned. He is clothed with beauty. The Lord is clothed with strength, and has girded Himself.

For he has established the world, which shall not be moved.
Your throne is prepared from of old. You are from everlasting.

The floods have lifted up, O Lord, the floods have lifted up their voices.
The floods have lifted up their waves, with the noise of many waters.

Wonderful are the surges of the sea; wonderful is the Lord on high.
Your testimonies become exceedingly credible; holiness becomes Your house, O Lord, unto length of days.

Glory be to the Father, and to the Son, and to the Holy Spirit.

As it was in the beginning, is now and ever shall be, world without end. Amen.

Antiphon: Wisdom has built her a house, she has mingled her wine, she has also furnished her table.
(At Easter time add—Alleluia.)

Antiphon: You did feed Your own people with Angels' food, and did send them bread from heaven.
(At Easter time add—Alleluia.)

Sing joyfully to God, all the earth. Serve you the Lord with gladness.
Come in before His presence, with exceedingly great joy.

Know you that the Lord He is God, He made us, and not we ourselves.

We are His people and the sheep of His pasture.

Go you into His gates with praise, into His courts with hymns and give glory to Him.

Praise you His name, for the Lord is sweet, His mercy endures forever, and His truth to generation and generation.

Glory be to the Father, and to the Son, and to the Holy Spirit.

As it was in the beginning, is now, and ever shall be, world without end. Amen.

Antiphon: You did feed Your own people with Angels' food, and did send them bread from heaven. (At Easter time add—Alleluia.)

Antiphon: The bread of Christ is fat and He shall serve dainties to kings. (At Easter time add—Alleluia.)

O God, my God, to you do I watch at break of day.

For You my soul has thirsted, for You my flesh, O how many ways!

In a desert land, and where there is no way and no water, so in the sanctuary have I come before You, to see Your power and Your glory.

For Your mercy is better than lives. You my lips shall praise.

So will I bless You all my life long, and in Your name I will lift up my hands.

Let my soul be filled as with marrow and fatness, and my mouth will praise You with joyful lips.

If I have remembered You upon my bed, I will meditate on You in the morning, because You have been my helper.

And I will rejoice under the cover of Your wings; my soul has stuck close to You; Your right hand has received me.

But they have sought my soul in vain, they shall go into the lower parts of the earth, they shall be delivered into the hands of the sword, they shall be the portion of foxes.

But the king shall rejoice in God, all they shall be praised that swear by Him, because the mouth is stopped of them that speak wicked things.

Glory be to the Father, and to the Son, and to the Holy Spirit.

As it was in the beginning, is now and ever shall be, world without end. Amen.

Antiphon: The bread of Christ is fat and he shall serve dainties to kings. (At Easter time add—Alleluia.)

Offer incense and bread to God. All you works of the Lord, bless the Lord.

Praise and exalt Him above all forever.

O you Angels of the Lord, bless the Lord. O you heavens, bless the Lord.

O all you waters that are above the heavens, bless the Lord.

O all you powers of the Lord, bless the Lord.

O you sun and moon, bless the Lord.

O you stars of heaven, bless the Lord. O shower and dew, bless the Lord.

O all you spirits of God, bless the Lord.

O you fire and heat, bless the Lord. O you cold and heat, bless the Lord.

O you dews and hoar frost, bless the Lord. O you frost and cold, bless the Lord.

O you ice and snow, bless the Lord. O you nights and days, bless the Lord.

O you light and darkness, bless the Lord. O you lightnings and clouds bless the Lord.

O let the earth bless the Lord; let it praise and exalt Him above all forever.

O you mountain and hills, bless the Lord. O all you things that spring upon the earth, bless the Lord.

O you fountains, bless the Lord. O you seas and rivers, bless the Lord.

O you whales, and all that love in the waters, bless the Lord. O all you fowls of the air, bless the Lord.

O all you beasts and cattle, bless the Lord. O you sons of men, bless the Lord.

O let Israel bless the Lord; let him praise and exalt Him above all forever.

O you priests of the Lord, bless the Lord. O you servants of the Lord, bless the Lord.

O you spirits and souls of the just, bless the Lord. O you holy and humble of heart, bless the Lord.

O Ananias, Azarias and Misael, bless the Lord. praise Him and exalt Him above all forever.

Bless we the Father and the Son, and the Holy Spirit; let us praise and exalt Him above all forever.

Blessed are You, O Lord, in the firmament of heaven, and to be praised and glorified, and exalted above all forever.

Antiphon: Holy priests offer incense and bread to God. (At Easter time all—Alleluia.)

Antiphon: To him that overcomes will I give hidden manna and a new name. (At Easter time all—Alleluia.)

Praise you the Lord from the heavens.
Praise you Him in the high places.

Praise you Him, all His Angels; praise you Him, all His hosts.
Praise you Him, O sun and moon; praise Him, all you stars and light.

Praise Him, you heavens of heavens, and let all the waters that are above the heavens praise the name of the Lord.
For He spoke, and they were made. He commanded, and they were created.

He has established them forever, and for ages of age. He has made a decree and it shall not pass away.
Praise the Lord from the earth, you dragons, and all you deeps: fire, hail, snow, ice, stormy winds, which fulfill His word.

Mountains, and all hills, fruitful trees, and all cedars,
Beasts, and all cattle, serpents, and feathered fowls.

Kings of the earth, and all people; princes and all judges of the earth.
Young men, and maidens; let the old with the younger praise the name of the Lord, for His name alone is exalted.

The praise of Him is above heaven and earth, and He has exalted the horn of His people.

A hymn to all His saints: to the children of Israel, a people approaching Him.

Glory be to the Father, and to the Son, and to the Holy Spirit.

As it was in the beginning, is now, and ever shall be, world without end. Amen.

Antiphon: To him that overcomes, will I give hidden manna, and a new name.

Priest: Brethren, I have received of the Lord that which also I delivered unto you, that the Lord Jesus, the same night in which He was betrayed, took bread, and when He had given thanks, He broke it, and said: "Take, eat; this is My Body, which shall be given for you. this do in remembrance of Me" (I Cor. 11:23).

All: Thanks be to God.

HYMN:

Priest: The word of God proceeding forth,

The word of God proceeding forth,
Yet leaving not the Father's side,
And going to His work on earth,
Had reached at length life's even-tide.

By a disciple to be given,
To rivals for His blood a thirst;
Himself the very Bread of heaven,
He gave to His disciples first.

He gave Himself in either kind,
His Precious Flesh, His Precious Blood.
Of flesh and blood is man combined,
And He, of man, would be the Food.

In Birth, man's Fellow-man was He;
His Meat, while sitting at the board;
He died, his Ransomer to be;
He reigns, to be his Great Reward.

O Saving Victim, slain to bless!
Who openest heaven's bright gates to all!
The attacks of many a foe oppress;
Give strength in strife, and help in fall.

To God, the Three in One, ascend
All thanks and praise forevermore.
He grants the life that shall not end,
Upon the heavenly country's shore.

All: Amen.

He makes peace in thy borders.
(At Easter time all—Alleluia.)

And fills you with the finest of the wheat
(At Easter time all—Alleluia.)

Antiphon: I am the living bread, which came down
from heaven; if any man eat of this Bread he will
live forever. (At Easter time—add Alleluia.)

BENEDICTUS

Priest: Blessed be the Lord God of Israel,

All: Because He has visited and wrought the
redemption of His people:

And has raised up a horn of salvation to us, in
the house of David His servant;

As He spoke by the mouth of His holy prophets,
who are from the beginning.

Salvation from our enemies, and from the hand of
all that hate us,

To show mercy to our fathers, and to remember
His holy covenant.

The oath which He swore to Abraham our father,
that He would grant to us,

That being delivered from the hand of our enemies,
we may serve Him without fear.

In holiness and justice, before Him all our days.

And you, O child, shall be called the prophet of
the most High, for you shall go before the face of
the Lord to prepare His way:

To give knowledge of salvation to His people, unto
the remission of their sins,

Through the bowels of the mercy of our God in
which the Orient, from on high, has visited us.

To enlighten them that sit in darkness, and in the
shadow of death,

To direct our feet into the way of peace.

Glory be to the Father, and to the Son, and to
the Holy Spirit.

As it was in the beginning, is now, and ever shall
be, world without end. Amen.

Antiphon: I am the living Bread which came down
from heaven; if any man eat of this Bread he will
live forever. (At Easter time—add Alleluia.)

CLOSING PRAYERS

Priest: O Lord, hear my prayer.
All: And let my cry come unto You.

Priest: Let us pray. O God, Who under a wonderful Sacrament has left unto us a memorial of Your Passion, grant unto us, we beseech You, so reverently to handle the Sacred Mysteries of Your Body and Blood, that we may always feel within ourselves the fruit of Your redeeming work, Who lives and reigns with God the Father, in the unity of the Holy Spirit, one God, world without end.
All: Amen.

Priest: O Lord, hear my prayer
All: And let my cry come unto You.

Priest: Let us bless the Lord.
All: Thanks be to God.

Priest: May the souls of the faithful departed, through the mercy of God, rest in peace.
All: Amen.

All: Silently... OUR FATHER Amen.

Priest: May the Lord give unto us His peace.
All: And life everlasting. Amen.

PRAYER TO THE BLESSED MOTHER

Priest: Hail, Holy Queen, Mother of mercy!
All: Our life, our sweetness, and our hope; to You do we cry, poor banished children of Eve; to You do we send up our sighs, mourning and weeping in this valley of tears. Turn then, most gracious advocate, Your eyes of mercy toward us, and, after this our exile, show unto us the blessed fruit of Your womb, Jesus, O clement, O loving, O sweet Virgin Mary!

Priest: Pray for us, O holy Mother of God.
All: That we may be made worthy of the promises of Christ.

Priest: Let us pray.
All: O Almighty and everlasting God, Who, by the cooperation of the Holy Spirit, did make ready both the body and soul of the glorious Virgin and Mother Mary worthily to become a meet dwelling for Your Son, grant that as we rejoice in Her memory, so by Her loving intercession we may be delivered from the evils that continually hang over us, and finally from everlasting death, through the same Christ, our Lord. Amen.

Priest: May the divine assistance remain always with us.
All: And may the souls of the faithful departed, through the mercy of God, rest in peace. Amen.

Priest: May all praise,
All: Honor, power, and glory be rendered by all creatures to the most holy and undivided Trinity, to the sacred humanity of our Lord Jesus Christ, to the fruitful integrity of the most blessed and glorious Virgin Mary, and to all of the Saints in general; and may we obtain the remission of all our sins through endless ages. Amen.

Priest: Blessed is the womb of the Virgin Mary, which has borne the Son of the Eternal Father.
All: And blessed are the breasts which have nourished Christ, our Lord.

(Our Father and Hail Mary are recited silently.)

HYMN: HUMBLY WE ADORE THEE

1. Humbly we adore Thee, Christ Redeemer King;
Thou art Lord of heaven, Thou to whom we sing.

CHORUS: Christ, our God and brother, hear our
humble plea,
By this holy banquet, keep us joined to Thee.

2. God, the Mighty, Thou hast come, bearing gifts of
grace;
Son of Adam still Thou art, Savior of our race.
(repeat chorus)

3. Jesus, Lord, we thank Thee, for this wondrous
Bread.
In our land Thou dwellest. By Thee we are fed.
(repeat chorus)

4. We who share this mystery, in Thee are made one.
Every act we offer Thee, in Thy Name is done.
(repeat chorus)

5. Thou Who died to save us, live on as our light.
Though our eyes are blinded, yet our faith gives
sight. (repeat chorus)

6. Christ, do Thou be merciful, Lamb for sinners slain.
We in grief confess our guilt; cleanse our soul of
stain. (repeat chorus)

7. Make us one in loving Thee, one in mind and heart.
From this holy unity, let us not depart.
(repeat chorus)

WORLD CONSECRATION TO THE
IMMACULATE HEART OF MARY

Queen of the most holy Rosary, help of Christians, refuge of the human race, victorious in all the battles of God, we prostrate ourselves in supplication before Thy throne, in the sure hope of obtaining mercy and of receiving grace and timely aid in our present calamities, not through any merits of our own on which we do not rely, but only through the immense goodness of Thy Mother's Heart.

In Thee and in Thy Immaculate Heart, at this grave hour of human history, do we put our trust; to Thee we consecrate ourselves, not only with all of Holy Church, which is the Mystical Body of Thy Son Jesus, and which is suffering in so many of her members, being subjected to manifold tribulations and persecutions, but also with the whole world, torn by discords, agitated with hatred, the victim of its own iniquities.

Be thou moved by the sight of such material and moral degradation, such sorrows, such anguish, so many tormented souls in danger of eternal loss!

Do thou, O Mother of mercy, obtain for us from God a Christ-like reconciliation of the nations, as well as those graces which can convert souls of men in an instant, those graces which prepare the way and make certain the long desired coming of peace on earth.

O Queen of peace, pray for us, and grant peace unto the world in the truth, the justice, and the charity of Christ.

Above all, give us peace in our hearts, so that the kingdom of God may spread its borders in the tranquility of order. Accord Thy protection to unbelievers, and to all those who lie within the shadow of death. Cause the Sun of Truth to rise upon them; may they be enabled to join with us in repeating before the Savior of the world: "Glory to God in the highest, and on earth peace to men of good will."

Give peace to nations that are separated from us by error or discord, and in a special manner to those peoples who profess a singular devotion toward Thee;

bring them back to Christ's one fold, under the one
true Shepherd.

Obtain full freedom for the Holy Church of God;
defend her from her enemies; check the ever increasing
torrent of immorality; arouse in the faithful a love of
purity, a practical Christian life, and an apostolic zeal,
so that the multitude of those who serve God may
increase in merit and in number.

Finally, even as the Church and all mankind were
once consecrated to the Heart of Thy Son, Jesus,
because He was, for all those who put their hope
in Him, an inexhaustible source of victory and
salvation, so in like manner do we consecrate
ourselves forever to Thee also, and to Thy Immaculate
Heart, O Mother of us and Queen of the World.

May Thy love and patronage hasten the day when
the kingdom of God shall be victorious and all the
nations, at peace with God and with one another, shall
call Thee blessed and intone with Thee, from the
rising of the sun to its going down, the everlasting
"Magnificat" of glory, of love, of gratitude to the Heart
of Jesus, in which alone we can find truth, life, and
peace.

LITANY OF THE BLESSED VIRGIN MARY

Lord, have mercy on us.
  (response) Christ, have mercy on us.
Lord, have mercy on us. Christ, hear us.
  (response) Christ, graciously hear us.

God the Father of Heaven, (Have mercy on us.)
God the Son, Redeemer of the world,
  (Have mercy on us.)
God the Holy Spirit, (Have mercy on us.)
Holy Trinity, One God, (Have mercy on us.)

Holy Mary, (Pray for us.)
Holy Mother of God,
Holy Virgin of virgins,   (Pray for us.)
Mother of Christ,

Mother of divine grace, (Pray for us.)
Mother most pure,
Mother most chaste,
Mother inviolate,
Mother undefiled,
Mother most amiable,
Mother most admirable,
Mother of good counsel,
Mother of our Creator,
Mother of our Savior,
Virgin most prudent,   (Pray for us.)
Virgin most venerable,
Virgin most renowned,
Virgin most powerful,
Virgin most merciful,
Virgin most faithful,
Mirror of justice,
Seat of wisdom,
Cause of our joy,
Spiritual vessel,
Vessel of honor,
Singular vessel of devotion,
Mystical rose,
Tower of David,
Tower of ivory,
House of gold,
Ark of the covenant,
Gate of heaven,
Morning star,
Health of the sick,
Refuge of sinners,
Comforter of the afflicted,
Help of Christians,
Queen of angels, (Pray for us.)
Queen of Patriarchs,
Queen of Prophets,
Queen of Apostles,
Queen of Martyrs,

Queen of Confessors,
Queen of Virgins, (Pray for us.)
Queen of all Saints,
Queen conceived without original sin,
Queen assumed into heaven,
Queen of the most holy Rosary,
Queen of the family,
Queen of Peace,

Lamb of God, who takes away the sins of the world, (spare us, O Lord)!
Lamb of God, who takes away the sins of the world, (graciously hear us, O Lord)!
Lamb of God, who takes away the sins of the world, (have mercy on us)!

Priest: Pray for us, O holy Mother of God.
All: That we may be made worthy of the promises of Christ.

BENEDICTION

HYMN: "DOWN IN ADORATION"

(TANTUM ERGO SACRAMENTUM)

Down in adoration falling,
Lo! the Sacred Host we hail;
Lo! o'er ancient forms departing,
Newer rites of grace prevail,
Faith for all defects supplying,
Where the feeble senses fail.
To the everlasting Father,
And the Son who reigns on high,
With the Holy Ghost proceeding
Forth from Each eternally.
Be salvation, honor, blessing,
Might, and endless majesty. Amen.

Priest: You have given them bread from heaven.
All: Having all sweetness within it.

THE DIVINE PRAISES

Blessed be God,
Blessed be His holy name.
Blessed be Jesus Christ, true God and true man.
Blessed be the name of Jesus.
Blessed be His most sacred heart.
Blessed be His most precious blood.
Blessed be Jesus in the most holy sacrament of the
altar.
Blessed be the Holy Spirit, the Paraclete.
Blessed be the great Mother of God, Mary most holy.
Blessed be Her holy and immaculate conception.
Blessed be Her glorious assumption.
Blessed be the name of Mary, Virgin and Mother.
Blessed be Saint Joseph, Her most chaste spouse.
Blessed be God in His angels and in His saints.

Brief Rosary Meditations

"My soul is sad, even unto death.
Wait here and watch with Me" (Matt. 26:38).

Joyful Mysteries (said on Monday and Thursday,
and Sunday in Advent)

1 Decade—The Annunciation
    Submission to God
2 Decade—The Visitation
    Love of our neighbor
3 Decade—The Nativity
    Humility
4 Decade—The Presentation of Our Lord
    Chastity and Obedience
5 Decade—The Finding of Our Lord
    Fidelity to our duties

Sorrowful Mysteries (said on Tuesday and Friday, and Sunday in Lent)

1 Decade—Agony of Our Lord
   Contrition for our sins
2 Decade—Scourging of Our Lord
   Mortification of the senses
3 Decade—Crowning with Thorns
   Disregard of human respect
4 Decade—Carrying of the Cross
   Patience in our trials
5 Decade—Crucifixion
   Pardon of injuries

Glorious Mysteries (said on Wednesday & Saturday, and Sunday, other than Advent and Lent)

1 Decade—Resurrection of Our Lord
   Love of prayer
2 Decade—Ascension
   Desire of Heaven
3 Decade—Descent of the Holy Spirit
   Gifts of the Holy Spirit
4 Decade—Assumption of Mary
   Grace of a happy death
5 Decade—Coronation of Mary
   Filial devotion to Mary

Prayer of the Pious Union

There is one special prayer that originated with the "Pious Union of the Holy Nights" which was founded in Bologna, Italy, in 1933. This was taken up by the Holy Capuchin priest, Father Pio of San Giovanni Rotondo in Italy, Those who join the "Pious Union of the Holy Nights" make an all night vigil, and the special prayer of the Pious Union is enough to provide adequate meditation even for an entire night.

O Jesus, who, in the excess of Your love to win hearts, does give abundant graces to those who meditate and diffuse devotion to your Holy Passion in Gethsemane, I pray You to lead my heart and soul to think often of the most bitter agony You suffered in the garden, to pity You and to join with You completely.

O most Holy Jesus, who bore during that night the weight of all our sins and paid for them, please grant me the great gift of perfect contrition for my many sins which caused You to sweat blood.

Most Holy Jesus, by virtue of the terrible struggle you endured in Gethsemane, give me the power of complete and final victory in the temptations that beset me, especially those to which I am most often subject.

O My Jesus, by virtue of the anxieties, fears, and the unknown but intense pain which You suffered on the night in which You were betrayed, give me the light to follow your Holy will, and to think upon and to understand the enormous effort and formidable struggle You endured victoriously in fulfilling, not Your will, but the will of the Father.

Praise to You, O Jesus, for the agony and the tears poured out during this holy night, from a dear and holy Jesus, for the sweat of blood and the deadly distress You endured that solitude, more frightful than man can imagine.

Praise to You, most sweet but vastly sorrowful Jesus, for the prayer at once human and divine which poured forth out from Your agonized Heart during that night of ingratitude and of treason.

Eternal Father, I offer to You all the Holy Masses of this moment, of the past, and of the future, united with Jesus in agony in the Garden of Olives.

O Most Holy Trinity, cause the knowledge and love of the Sacred Passion of Gethsemane to be diffused in the world.

And, O My Jesus, may those who love You and look upon the crucifix, remember Your incredible pain in the garden, and may they follow Your example, learn to pray well, to fight and overcome, so they may eternally glorify You in heaven. Amen.

Special Vigil in Honor of God the Father

At first it seems almost unbelievable that a world-shaking message from God the Father given in 1932, and fully approved by the Church, was never translated into English until 1996.

However this message, given so long ago to the general superior of a congregation of women in Grenoble, France, is especially timely. (An Italian edition of the messages was published in Rome in March, 1989, with imprimatur of the Most Rev. Peter Canisius van Lierde, Vicar General of Vatican City. The first English edition was printed August 7, 1996.)

The first bishop to approve the messages said that, "humanly speaking" it would be difficult to explain that this message came from a nun not trained in theology. He added that "the object of her mission (for a more intimate devotion to God as our Father) is precise and, from the doctrinal point of view...legitimate and *timely*." (From the pastoral letter of Most Rev. A. Caillot, Bishop of Grenoble, after a ten year inquiry which began in 1935.)

Our Father revealed: "The joy I feel in being with you is no less great than that which I felt when I was with My Son, Jesus, during His mortal life. My Son...it was I Who sent Him. He was conceived by My Holy Spirit, Who I Myself am. In a word, I was always I."

"I Will Come Very Close"

He asks that all men realize that He is a *loving* Father Who has been revealed to us by His Son. "My presence among you is like the sun on the earth. If you are well disposed to receive Me, I will come very close to you, enter into you, light you up and warm you with My Infinite Love."

As a loving Father He deplores that so many in the world do not know him, and so many fear Him. He said: "I desire to be known by all of you so that you can all enjoy, even here on earth, My goodness and My tenderness. Make yourselves apostles to those who still do not know Me, and I will bless your toil and efforts, preparing great glory for you with Me in eternity!"

He said that if men only knew that He was truly their loving Father, "conversions would be more numerous and persevering." He promised that all who call Him "Father" (with realization that this, indeed, He is) *will be sure of their eternal life among the chosen ones.*"

Following is part of a most beautiful prayer given by our Father:

My Father, since it is Your wish that we should always turn to You, I come with confidence to ask You, together with Jesus and Mary...(request the favor you desire).

For this intention, and uniting myself to their Most Sacred Hearts, I offer all my prayers, my sacrifices and mortifications, all my actions, and greater faithfulness to my duties.

Give me the light, the grace, and the power of the Holy Spirit! Strengthen me in this Spirit that I may never lose Him, never sadden Him, and never allow Him to become weaker in me.

My Father, I ask this in the name of Jesus, Your Son! And You, Jesus, open Your Heart and place in It my own and, together with Mary's, offer it to our Divine Father! Obtain for me the grace that I need!

(If the above prayer is to be recited as a novena, add: "I promise to be more generous, especially during these nine days, in a given circumstance, to such and such a person...")

This excerpt from the prayer taught to the world by God the Father *highlights devotion to the **Sacred Hearts** with simplicity and clarity.*

How beautiful is that invitation of our Father to pray: *"Jesus, open Your Heart and place in It my own and, together with Mary's, offer it to our Divine Father!"* Is this not a summary of all we have been saying in this little book, *Night of Love?* Is this not the heart of the Divine message for our times?

Following are the beautiful prayers taught by our loving Father and *the meditations on the Rosary which He gave.* For this vigil we recommend the use of the book, *The Father Speaks to His Children.*

"Through Him, with Him, and in Him," God is My Father

My Father in Heaven, how sweet it is to know that You are my Father and that I am Your child!

Especially when the skies of my soul are cloudy and my cross weighs more heavily, I feel the need to repeat to You: Father, I believe in Your love for me!

Yes, I believe that You are a Father to me at every moment of my life, and that I am Your child!

I believe that You love me with an infinite love!

I believe that You are watching over me night and day, and that not a hair falls from my head without Your permission!

I believe that, in Your infinite Wisdom, You know better than I what is good for me.

I believe that, in Your infinite power, You can bring good, even out of evil.

I believe that, in Your infinite goodness, You make everything to the advantage of those who love You; even under the hands of those who strike me, I kiss Your hand which heals!

I believe, but increase in me faith, hope, and love!

Teach me always to see Your love as my guide in every event my life.

Teach me to surrender myself to You like a baby in its mother's arms.

Father, You know everything. You see everything, You know me better than I know myself; You can do everything, and You love me!

My Father, since it is Your wish that we should always turn to You, I come with confidence to ask You, together with Jesus and Mary...(request the favor that you desire).

For this intention, and uniting myself to their Most Sacred Hearts, I offer You all my prayers, my sacrifices and mortifications, all my actions, and greater faithfulness to my duties.

Give me the light, the grace, and the power of the Holy Spirit!

Strengthen me in this Spirit, that I may never lose Him, never sadden Him, and never allow Him to become weaker in me.

My Father, I ask this in the name of Jesus, Your Son! And You, Jesus, open Your Heart and place in It my own, and together with Mary's, offer It to our Divine Father! Obtain for me the grace that I need!

Divine Father, call all men to Yourself. Let all the world proclaim Your Fatherly Goodness and Your Divine Mercy!

Be a tender Father to me and protect me wherever I am, like the apple of Your eye. Make me always a worthy son or daughter; have mercy on me!

Divine Father, sweet hope of our souls, may You be known, honored, and loved by all men!

Divine Father, infinite goodness poured out on all peoples, may You be known, honored, and loved by all men!

Divine Father, beneficent dew of humanity, may You be known, honored, and loved by all men!

THE ROSARY OF THE FATHER

O God, come to save me.
Lord, come soon to my help.
Glory be to the Father...

My good Father, I offer myself to Thee.
Angel of God, my guardian dear, to whom His love commits me here, ever this day be at my side, to light and guard, to rule and guide.

In the first mystery, we contemplate *the triumph of the Father in the garden of Eden,* when, after the sin of Adam and Eve, He promises the coming of the Lord.

And the Lord God said to the serpent: "Because thou hast done this thing, thou art cursed among all cattle, and beasts of the earth: upon thy breast shalt thou go, and earth shalt thou eat all the days of thy life. I will put enmity between thee and the Woman, and thy seed and Her seed: She shall crush thy head, and thou shalt lie in wait for Her heel" (Gen. 3:14-15).

One Hail Mary, ten Our Fathers, Glory be...
My Good Father... Angel of God...

In the second mystery, we contemplate *the triumph of the Father at the moment of Mary's Fiat* during the Annunciation.

And the angel said to Her: "Fear not, Mary, for Thou hast found grace with God. Behold Thou shalt conceive in Thy womb, and shalt bring forth a son; and Thou shalt call His name Jesus. He shall be great, and shall be called the Son of the Most High; and the Lord God shall give unto Him the throne of David, His father; and He shall reign in the house of Jacob forever. And of His kingdom there shall be no end (Lk. 1:30-33).

One Hail Mary, ten Our Fathers, Glory be...
My Good Father... Angel of God...

In the third mystery, we contemplate *the triumph of the Father in the garden of Gethsemane* when He gives all His power to the Son.

...Father, if thou wilt, remove this chalice from me: but yet not my will, but thine be done. And there appeared to him an angel from heaven, strengthening him. And being in an agony, he prayed the longer. And his sweat became as drops of blood, trickling down upon the ground (Lk. 22:42-44).

One Hail Mary, ten Our Fathers, Glory be...
My Good Father... Angel of God...

155.

In the fourth mystery, we contemplate *the triumph of the Father at the moment of every particular judgment.*

And rising up he came to his father. And when he was yet a great way off, his father saw him, and was moved with compassion, and running to him fell upon his neck, and kissed him. And the son said to him: Father, I have sinned against heaven, and before thee, I am not now worthy to be called thy son. And the father said to his servants: Bring forth quickly the finest robe, and put it on him, and put a ring on his hand, and shoes on his feet. And bring hither the fatted calf, and kill it, and let us eat and make merry, because this my son was dead, and is come to life again, was lost, and is found. And they began to be merry (Lk. 15:20-24).

One Hail Mary, ten Our Fathers, Glory be...
My Good Father... Angel of God...

In the fifth mystery, we contemplate *the triumph of the Father in the final judgment.*

And I saw a new heaven and a new earth. For the first heaven and the first earth had passed away, and the sea was no more. And I, John, saw the holy city, the new Jerusalem, coming down out of heaven from God, prepared as a bride adorned for her husband. And I heard a great voice from the throne, saying: Behold the tabernacle of God with men, and He will dwell with them. And they shall be His people; and God Himself with them shall be their God. And God shall wipe away all tears from their eyes; and death shall be no more, nor mourning, nor crying, nor sorrow shall be any more, for the former things have passed away (Rev. 21:1-4).

One Hail Mary, ten Our Fathers, Glory be...
My Good Father... Angel of God...
Amen, amen.

LITANY OF THE FATHER

(After every phrase, respond, HAVE MERCY ON US)

O God, Father of Heaven, (have mercy on us).
O God, Son, Redeemer of the world,
O God, Holy Spirit,
Holy Trinity, one God,
Father, creator of the world,
Father, peacemaker of the world,
Father, eternal wisdom,
Father, infinite goodness,
Father, bountiful,
Father, fount of everything,
Father, most sweet,
Father, of infinite mercy,
Father, our defender,
Father, our glory and our happiness,
Father, wealth of all people,
Father, triumph of all nations,
Father, hope of all Christians,
Father, splendor of the Church,
Father, splendor of kings,
Father, overturner of idols,
Father, consolation of people,
Father, happiness of priests,
Father, guide of men,
Father, gift of family life,
Father, help of the poor,
Father, guide of youth,
Father, friend of children,
Father, freedom of slaves,
Father, light of those who are in darkness,
Father, destroyer of the proud,
Father, wisdom of the just,
Father, rest in tribulations,
Father, hope in desolation,
Father, harbor of safety in dangers,
Father, consolation of the poor,
Father, consolation of the afflicted,
Father, refuge of the hopeless,
Father, refuge of the orphans,
Father, refuge of the aged,
Father, refuge of the dying,

Father, that extinguishes our thirst and poverty,
Father, life of the dead,
Father, glory of the saints.

Lamb of God, You take away the sins of the world,
(forgive us, oh Lord).
Lamb of God, You take away the sins of the world,
(graciously hear us, oh Lord).
Lamb of God, You take away the sins of the world,
(have mercy on us).

FINAL PRAYER

Father, the earth needs You; every man needs You. The heavy and polluted air needs You. We beg You, dear Father, come back to walk through the streets of the world. Come back to live among Your people. Come back to guide the nations. Come back to bring peace and with it Your justice. Come back to bring the fire of Thy love. So...redeemed by sorrow, we can become new creatures. Amen, amen.

(All quotes above are from the booklet, *The Father Speaks to His Children* which can be obtained from the *Father of All Mankind Foundation*, 2171 Joy Road, Auburn Hills, MI 48326.

For a free copy of the complete prayer given by our Father, send a stamped and self-addressed envelope to LAF, P.O. Box 50, Asbury, NJ 08802.)

ADDITIONAL VIGIL SUGGESTIONS:

Henrietta Bower's Vigil Program

When we were preparing this handbook we wrote to all who had actively participated in the vigil movement for suggestions, especially for vigils which lacked priests or speakers.

One of the most competent persons to contribute ideas was Mrs. Henrietta Bower, who was in a sense the founder of the vigil movement in the English speaking world.

Mrs. Bower enumerated the following principles which should be incorporated in a vigil program given the unusual factor that there will not be outstanding speakers available for the entire night:

1) After one a.m., any talking by one person (even including priests) *should be limited* to three, or at the very most, five minutes at a time.

2) The program *should be flexible* to take advantage of personnel present. There is no reason why the program could not vary from time to time as long as it is kept interesting.

Sometimes an entirely new leader makes a tremendous impact, and if something of a duller nature has been planned for other parts of the vigil, this leader could be invited to fuller participation.

Local circumstances should be taken into consideration and utilized, as on a special feast, or in some special place.

Usually vigilers chat in the coffee breaks and become acquainted. But it seemed appropriate at Knock in Ireland when priests put the pilgrims in absolute silence for the night even during the break, saying that it is through silence that the "knocking of prayers" will be heard. (Knock is the one place where Our Lady appeared and never spoke; her message was conveyed through the imagery of the vision which showed the unity of Calvary with the Mass).

Earlier vigils in England were known simply as "Rosary Vigils," and when there was no priest present, different laymen led the Rosary, announcing intentions before each decade. Many ideas came up from the laity spontaneously, so long as they had a definite intention for the decade, such as praying for the suffering Church of silence. This is the program Mrs. Bower first suggested for general use. But when English vigilers began to go frequently to Lourdes a more detailed program was adopted.

4) Finally and importantly, there must be movement at regular intervals (standing, kneeling, moving in turn) regardless of what prayers are used.

Program Used at Lourdes
(Also Suitable to Fatima and Other Shrines)

A Blessed Sacrament Father from the midlands of England, who had accompanied the English vigilers to Lourdes a number of times, published an all night vigil prayer book with a full text of all the prayers he had chosen to be used during the night. "He must have put hours of work into it," Mrs. Bower remarked. "I am looking at some of the psalms for the conversion of Russia he has chosen—67 and 73—followed by quotes from the Acts of the Apostles 111, verses 13 to 25."

Mrs. Bower's own suggestion for a program (used at the Grotto at Lourdes) follows:

1) (kneeling) O Salutaris

2) (kneeling) Prayer for those now making the vigil an Act of Consecration to the Sacred Heart,

3) (standing) Hymn—O Godhead Hid

4) (kneeling) Act of Consecration to the Immaculate Heart of Mary

5) (sitting) Explanation of vigil program (allow 5 minutes). This explanation is divided into 3 parts:

    a) division into groups: names of priest leaders, names of couriers;

    b) announcement of program which is to follow;

    c) any other notices concerning spiritual part of vigil such as indulgences, time for Confessions, etc.

6) (kneeling) Prayers for deceased vigil members and past vigil members

7) (standing) Hymn

8) (sitting) Explanation of all night vigil:

a) Its purpose in general;

b) Christian Unity in particular (allow 5 minutes)

9) (kneeling) Prayers for Christian Unity

10) (standing) Hymn

11) (sitting) Importance of the conversion of Russia (allow 5 minutes)

12) (kneeling) Prayers for the conversion of Russia

13) (standing) Hymn

14) (kneeling) Three Hail Marys for the Holy Father and the bishops of the world, three Hail Marys for the diocese in which the vigil is held

15) (sitting) Explanation of importance of prayers for persecuted Church (allow 5 minutes)

16) (kneeling) Prayers for Persecuted Church

17) (kneeling) *Tantum Ergo, Divine Praises, Adoremus in Aeternum*

18) (standing) *Faith of Our Fathers*

Advantage of Vigil at Shrine

At Lourdes, and Fatima, vigilers have the great advantage of being able to move from one location to another. They can have part of the Holy Hour at the place of the apparition, part in the Rosary Square, and a part in one of the other locations or chapels, with constant movement with silent prayer or singing between each. The next hour of their program is divided between a half hour in the church and a half hour at another location, as follows:

1) (sitting) Hymn

2) (sitting) Short talk on Introit of Mass (allow 5 minutes)

3) (kneeling) Litany

4) (walking around church) Part of Lourdes Hymn

5) (sitting) Talk on Epistle of the Mass (5 minutes)

6) (standing) Hymn

7) (kneeling) Anthem of Our Lady according to the season (said in English)

8) (sitting) Talk on Gospel of Mass (allow 5 minutes)

9) (kneeling) Private prayer (at most 3 minutes)

10) (standing) Hymn

Now with everyone thoroughly awake from the procession from the Church to the place of apparition, and of course of arriving in this holy place where Our Lady appeared, the next part of the vigil consisting of a half an hour follows:

1) (kneeling) Five decades of Rosary with either quotations from the Old Testament or from the New Testament

2) (walking) An act of penance, kissing the rock beneath statue at Lourdes, or the ground at Fatima, etc.

3) (kneeling and standing alternately) Decades of the Rosary as above.

Those who do not have the privilege of making a vigil at a Shrine could very likely make use of these suggestions in some way in their own parish churches by visiting side altars, venerating a relic of the patron saint of the church or of the particular patron of that vigil. Then they can move from the area of the side altar back to the center of the church, if this is feasible, around the side aisles.

Next Holy Hour

The next part of the vigil is the Holy Hour back in the church.

1) (kneeling) Prayers for sick

2) (walking around church) Litany, or a Psalm, or reading from New Testament

3) (sitting) Short talk (3 minutes)

4) (standing) Hymn

5) (kneeling) A spiritual Communion for one of three special intentions formulated just for this vigil

6) (walking around church) A Psalm connected with this particular intention

7) (sitting) Short talk (3 minutes)

8) (standing) Hymn

9) (kneeling) Prayers for the pilgrims' own intentions

10) (standing) Hymn

11) (sitting) Short talk (3 minutes)

12) (walking around church) Litany, reading or Psalm

13) (kneeling) Prayers for Christian Unity etc.

14) (standing) Hymn

15) (kneeling) Prayers for pilgrims' intentions

16) (sitting) Short talk (3 minutes)

17) (standing) Hymn

18) (kneeling) Prayers for deceased vigil members such as "Out of the depth," the Preface of the day's Mass, Post Communion prayer

19) (sitting) Short talk (3 minutes)

20) (walking around church) Litany or Psalm, selection of Invocations

21) (sitting) Short talk (3 minutes

22) (standing) Hymn

23) (kneeling) Private prayer, 5 minutes at most)

24) (standing) Hymn

Program in Parishes

Those who are making use of the parish church can move to another area, can have a procession of Our Lady's statue, or even have a procession to some outdoor shrine, weather permitting, which is usually to be found at most churches.

1) (alternately kneeling and standing) The last five decades of the Rosary, using spontaneous meditations or quotations from the Old and New Testaments.

2) (standing) Recall Apparitions and give act of penance

3) (sitting) Short talk (5 minutes)

4) Continuation of the decades of the Rosary

When doing this Rosary decade at Lourdes the group is able to touch the rock on which Our Lady appeared, to kneel where Bernadette knelt, etc., and this adds a great deal to the spirit of devotion, especially with these pilgrims who have come all the way from England just for this night to this very holy place, and who may not have come before or hope to come again.

Now comes an hour which, at Lourdes and Fatima, the vigilers spend in the Rosary Square.

Stations of the Cross

Walking is necessary as they make the Stations of the Cross, with everyone reading the meditations together. If the weather is cold, as it often is at Lourdes at night, the program includes brisk movements between the Stations.

1) (standing) Hymn

2) (kneeling) Prayers for Church of Silence

3) (standing) Three-minute talk on how the all-night vigil fulfills the modern requests made by Our Lady for prayer and penance at Lourdes and Fatima

4) (walking around church) Psalm for Persecuted Church

5) (kneeling) Prayers for Priests

6) (sitting) Short talk (3 minutes)

7) (standing) Hymn

8) (kneeling) Prayers for Christian Unity

9) (walking) Psalm for Christian Unity and hymn

10) (sitting) Short talk (3 minutes)

11) (kneeling) Litany

12) (standing) Hymn

13) (kneeling) Psalm for conversion of Russia

14) (sitting) Short talk (3 minutes)

15) (kneeling) Private prayer (3 minutes)

16) (standing) Hymn

17) (kneeling) *Tantum Ergo*; prayers for our nation; *Divine Praises; Adoremus in Aeternum.*

It is suggested that all prayers, litanies, Psalms, and readings from the New Testament be recited together.

Sometimes the last Holy Hour will be shortened, owing to the time of the morning Mass. If this is so, then prayers to be said during this shortened hour should be those of the group Holy Hour.

Priests

It seems to have been a rather common history of the vigil movement that although it might begin with a few lay persons spending the night together, the priests joined in increasing numbers until it was even possible to have a different priest for every hour and even a different priest for every address.

Of course a priest is absolutely indispensable for the opening Mass in the evening, for the procession of the Blessed Sacrament, and for the closing Benediction and morning Mass.

But even as it is fitting and in the spirit of the new Liturgy for laymen to read publicly during the early part of the Mass, so it is particularly fitting that laymen should read and speak during the vigil. Fortunate indeed is the vigil group which has a strong-minded and capable leader who can enforce fitting variations of the vigil program with understanding and wisdom, utilizing the best possible talents of the whole vigil group so that this will be a night which all will remember, a night of charisms, a night of intimacy with Our Lord in the Eucharist, a night which ends not in growing fatigue, but climaxing in increased devotion and divine love.

Concluding Remarks

Do not forget the element of MOVEMENT, preferably several times in the same hour. *Use as many as four speakers for a meditation if necessary,* and let them rather be speakers than readers. Use the THOUGHTS rather than the words. Have at least one procession each hour. Some may say that there should be long periods of absolute silence for Eucharistic adoration, but most lay persons are not accustomed to more than a few minutes of unaided, silent prayer.

Some also say we should not take up so much of the night with the Rosary, but we think actual use of the meditations found in Part II will answer that objection. Cardinal O'Connor of New York, who inaugurated the vigils at St. Patrick's Cathedral in America's greatest metropolis, said:

"It is appropriate to have the recitation of the Rosary in the all night vigil. Jesus in the Eucharist is the very same Person Who was conceived in the womb of Mary." He added: "Mysteriously, spiritually, Christ comes forth on this altar because mysteriously, spiritually, Mary says, 'yes.'"

Eucharistic Prayer of Akita

Most Sacred Heart of Jesus, TRULY present in the Holy Eucharist, I consecrate my body and soul to be entirely one with Your Heart, being sacrificed at every instant on all the altars of the world, and giving praise to the Father, pleading for the coming of His Kingdom. Please receive this humble offering of myself. Use me as You will for the glory of the Father and the salvation of souls.

Most Holy Mother of God, never let me be separated from Your Divine Son. Please defend and protect me as Your special child. Amen.

Meditate Upon

The Seven Sorrows Of Mary

1) The prophecy of Simeon.

2) The flight into Egypt.

3) The loss of the Child Jesus in the temple.

4) The meeting of Jesus and Mary on the way to Calvary.

5) The Crucifixion.

6) The taking down of the Body of Jesus from the Cross.

7) The burial of Jesus.

Sorrowful and Immaculate Heart of Mary,
pray for us who have recourse to Thee.

Books by John M. Haffert:

1) *Mary In Her Scapular Promise (Sign Of Her Heart)* —
1940, 1942, 1954
2) *From A Morning Prayer (The Brother And I)* —
1941, 1971
3) *A Letter From Lisieux* — 1942
4) *The Peacemaker Who Went To War* — 1946
5) *Russia Will Be Converted* — 1950, 1956
6) *Meet The Witnesses* — 1961
7) *Queen's Promise* — 1966
8) *Night Of Love* — 1966, 1997
9) *The World's Greatest Secret* —1967, 1985, 1996
10) *Sex And The Mysteries* — 1970
11) *Explosion Of The Supernatural* —1975, 1996
12) *Dear Bishop!* —1982
13) *Who Is The Woman Of The Apocalypse?* — 1983
14) *The Hand Of Fatima* — 1984
15) *Go! Your Mother Is Calling* — 1986
16) *The Meaning Of Akita* — 1989
17) *Her Own Words* — 1993
18) *To Prevent This!* —1993
19) *Finally Russia!* — 1993
20) *Her Glorious Title* — 1993
21) *You, Too! Go Into The Vineyard* — 1995, 1996
22) *Now The Woman Shall Conquer* — 1997

Editor of *The Scapular* Magazine — 1941 to 1948
Editor of *Soul* Magazine — 1950 to 1987
Editor of *Voice Of The Sacred Hearts* Magazine —
1993 to 1996

Translations with Commentary:

Akita — The Tears and Message of Mary, —1989
by Fr. Teiji Yasuda

What Happened At Pontmain, — 1971
by Abbe Richard

*(Contact the 101 Foundation
for information about obtaining these books.)*